DAY OF OCTAGON

WORKS BY TY'RON W. C. ROBINSON II

<u>BOOKS</u>

DARK TITAN UNIVERSE SAGA

MAIN SERIES

Dark Titan Knights
The Resistance Protocol
Tales of the Scattered
Tales of the Numinous
Day of Octagon
Crossbreed (Forthcoming)
Heaven's Called (Forthcoming)

SPIN-OFFS

In A Glass of Dawn: The Casebook of Travis Vail
Maveth: Bloodsport (Forthcoming)
Maveth: Bloodsport (Forthcoming)
The Curse of The Mutant-Thing (Forthcoming)
Trail of Vengeance (Forthcoming)
War of the Thunder Gods (Forthcoming)

COLLECTED EDITIONS

Dark Titan Omnibus: Volume. 1
Dark Titan One-Shot Collection
The Swordman Collection
The Commander Norland Collection
The Chosen Son Collection
The Nano Man Collection

THE HAUNTED CITY SAGA

The Legendary Warslinger: The Haunted City I
Battle of Astolat: A Haunted City Prequel (KOBO Exclusive/Forthcoming)
Redemption of the Lost: The Haunted City II (Forthcoming)
Consequences of the Suffering: The Haunted City III (Forthcoming)

SYMBOLUM VENATORES SERIES

Symbolum Venaores: The Gabriel Kane Collection
Hod

OTHER BOOKS

Lost in Shadows: A Novel
Lost in Shadows: Remastered
Accounts of The Dead Days
The Book of The Elect
Hallow Sword: Cursed(KOBO Exclusive)
Dark Titan Parables Collection

DAY OF OCTAGON

TY'RON W. C. ROBINSON II

CONTENTS

HALLOW SWORD: WAR GAMES

I

<u>CONFLICT ON THE STREETS</u>

The city of Retropolis, after being invaded by what the people have called, "*beings from the sky*", is near rebuilt to what it once was before the invasion and the formation of The Resistance. Now, during the city's rebuilding process, Sir Onyx and J have come to a disagreement concerning the use of crime throughout the city. Both have declared war onto one another and have begun the battles in the streets of Retropolis.

Citizens are fleeing the areas invaded by the gangs of Onyx and J. most of the lower-class areas of the city are now in the hands of either Onyx or J. most of the upper-class areas are secured by the armed forces that have entered the city since the aftermath of its battle. On the outskirts of the city, within the Swordlair, The Swordman sits and stares at the computer monitor, watching and witnessing the turf war unfold between Onyx and J. Allison walks into the Swordlair from its entrance, coming down its stairs and seeing Kenari at the desk and monitor.

"What has become of the city?"

"It is what it has always been." Kenari said. "A place for the wicked to dwell."

"It is something. To have a figure like yourself to roam the city during its night hours and yet, the people believed you to be a mythic being."

"Some still do. Its best to keep it that way."

"But, many saw you on the streets during the Battle of Retropolis. Aligned with the other heroes. You possibly can't believe that many people disbelieve after witnessing that."

"The media is used for control and they can manipulate whatever they wish. Only a few will believe The Swordman's existence. Others will count it as a urban myth."

"I take it you're going out there to see what's really taking place?"

"It is my duty as The Swordman."

He prepped himself and grabbed his sword, placing on his hood, he entered The *Land-Dagger*. Driving out of the Swordlair toward the city of Retropolis.

In an office building, Elliot Slade and Ramon Lamano Carr have themselves a meeting. Both are frightened and serious concerning their conversation and where it's heading between the two of them. Words being used in ways foreign to their own ears. Choosing sides and opposing forces within the criminal underworld.

"I say we should align with Onyx." Slade declared. "He's basically new to the place and he has ideas that would make us wealthy in this city."

"I understand your point of view, Elliot. I really do. But, I feel that J has been here longer than Onyx and he knows this city from the inside out. Plus, he has history with The Swordman. Something that Onyx does not fully possess."

"Onyx knows what The Swordman can do. Remember the warehouse, where The Swordman came through and confronted Onyx. Onyx knows about The Swordman and that event created history between them."

"It's not enough history to grasp onto."

Slade shook his head and looked at Ramon.

"Look, its best we pick one of them now. Because if we don't, it's possible both will come looking for us. It won't be a pleasant visit for sure."

Ramon nodded as he drank his glass of whiskey.

"You have a point there. Best we make our decisions now or face our untimely death within the coming days. Hell, we already know how they operate."

In the lower-class area of Retropolis, the gang war between Onyx and J continued. Within them firing rounds of ammo against each other. Both of their gangs fighting each other in the rainy streets. Onyx and J stand in the streets with their gangs behind them. Staring down one another with firearms in their hands. J has his sword on his side.

"You could've accepted my terms, Conley!" Onyx shouted. "But, you chose death over life!"

"I made the decision that was best for me and my order. I know this city much more than you do, and I know how it should operate."

"If you believe what you're speaking, take me out now and end this turf war of ours before more people die because of your lack of understanding!"

"I will not kill you in this manner, Onyx."

Onyx nodded and pointed his finger at J. laughing to himself as he raised up a machine gun toward J.

"Then, I'll just do it!"

Onyx fired the machine gun at J, who ducked down and moved out of the gun's range. Hiding behind the sets of cars that are around them. Onyx continued to fire the machine gun and it ran out of ammo. Onyx went to reload the machine gun and he felt a presence around their location. Onyx looked and seen J looking up down the street, Onyx did the same and they both could see the Land-Dagger approaching.

"Here he comes." J said.

"Not now!" Onyx yelled with stress.

Both ran toward their cars as The Swordman elevated out of the moving vehicle, into the streets. Dressed in his black and dark grey ninja-esque uniform.

"We have to go now!" Onyx yelled at his driver.

The Swordman landed on the streets, fighting off the gang members that rushed toward him. Onyx and J escaped the location in their own cars, though chasing down each other in a fashion of a speed chase. The Swordman gazed around, Onyx and J escaped with some of their men and the others laid out on the pavement of the streets. He looked around, spotting one of Onyx's gang members crouched near a dumpster. The Swordman approached the gang member and grabbed him by his throat, slamming him against the brick building he stood next to.

"Tell me what is going on between Onyx and J?" The

Swordman asked.

"I'm not telling you anything!"

The gang member went for a punch, but The Swordman caught his fist and slammed him onto the ground, stomped his foot on the gang member's face. The gang member struggled to get out of the hold, but he could not.

"You will answer my question or you might not have a face anymore."

"Ok! Ok! Sir Onyx and J were supposed to make an agreement with each other about which districts of Retropolis they would control. But, they had a disagreement and it turned into a turf war. Now, our orders are to find and kill anyone who is aligned with J or face death ourselves at Sir Onyx's hand."

"What about facing death at my hand? Your boss didn't tell you what I did to his other soldiers before."

"He told us and that is why we had to keep this on a low profile. But, now you know and they know you will come for them."

"That I will do."

The Swordman slammed his knee onto the gang member's head, knocking him out. He jumped into his car and drove away from the area.

II

<u>WAR GAMES BEGIN</u>

The Swordman returned to the Swordlair, wherein awaiting him are two of his childhood friends and members of The Order of Swords. Kimmiko Vantez and Kinero Danforth. Kimmiko, known in the urban myths as Gozen while Kinero is referred to as Firebolt. Parking the Land-Dagger, Swordman exited the car, removing his hood and mask and approached his friends.

"It is something to see the two of you here." Kenari said, hugging them both.

"We came on some very important business." Kimmiko said. "And we're here to have your assistance."

"What kind of business would this be?"

"I think you know what it is, brother." Kinero mentioned. "We have received word regarding a turf war between two gangs and we're here to cease it."

"Good to know. I have already spoken with one of their men. Je gave me some information regarding this turf war. I will say it will require your help."

"What can we do?" Kimmiko asked.

"It would be for the best for the two of you to scout the surrounding locations of the turf war. Find out where the bases are for both Sir Onyx and J."

"We know J, but who is Sir Onyx?"

"He's new to the area. Came from the States."

"So, what about you?" Kimmiko asked. "What are you going to do while we're out scouting?"

"I have someone to meet and she will be of good use to us."

"You think she'll listen and work alongside us on this?"

"She assisted me with Onyx and J not too long ago, I believe she will do so again."

"Tell me this before we head out, Brother. Why do you continue to work alongside her when she's not even one of us. She declined the offer to be a part of us and the Creed. So, why do you still work with her after all of this?"

"Because her skills prove that she is useful in cases such as this. Whether or not she ever accepts or declines the offer, she will still be an asset."

Kinero nodded.

"I can understand your meaning, brother."

Kimmiko and Kinero left the Swordlair as Kenari sat at the computer table, searching for any signs of the Huntswoman in the past few hours.

Sir Onyx and his gang made their way to Rockward Penitentiary. Sneaking their way in to find more recruits for the turf war. One of the dirty cops escorted them down a corridor where they saw prisoners in their cells. Onyx measured them by their size and posing threats.

"I am sure that you can find some of these men useful for your war against J."

"I wouldn't bother about it." Onyx said. "Conley will be dealt with and the city will know who truly runs it.

"I will tell you that there is one man here who can do more than you might have asked for."

"Where is this man that you've spoken of?"

"He's right down here. Follow me, sir."

Onyx followed the cop down another hallway and stopped at an office. Within the office, the cop smiled while Onyx looked at the man, who sat in the chair facing the desk, staring at them.

"This is the guy." The cop said.

"Are you sure about him?"

"Very sure. He's here for a mission of his own. Sent by some person he called A.B."

In the same hour, J and his gang took a trip Pegasus Prison and within the walls of the large and mysterious prison, J spoke with a woman named Kimberly Jacobs, who only a few of the civilians known as the urban myth Fear. J and Kimberly entered a secure office and J's guards kept watch from the outside. The two sat at a table.

"You know why I've come here." J said. "You know what is happening out there."

"I've heard the rumors and I've seen some things. How those '*Beings from the Sky*' came down and wreaked havoc. I also saw those who fought against them. That moment told me this world is much bigger than what the average man or woman believes it to be."

"The Battle of Retropolis opened the door for me to spread my domain and my ruler ship of the underground."

"So, you're here to find some recruits or just a recruit."

"Something of that nature. I believe there is someone or some people here that can help me achieve my goal. My associate has already told me of Sir Onyx searching for recruits over at Rockward. Which is why I came here."

"Then, you've chosen the right place."

"How can I be sure of your words?"

"Because, you're talking with me for starters and I know lots of some ones that can be of great use for your goal being accomplished."

"Give me some names."

"I'll rather just show you. Come with me."

The office door opened, and Kimberly leads J down toward a particular room. There, J saw a man, wearing all armor with the colors of dark blue and grey. His face could be seen as he removed his helmet, He pointed with certainty in his eyes and Kimberly looked ahead, seeing the armored man being thanked by the Pegasus guards. She smiled.

"Who is he?" J asked.

"Why, he just came in to deliver someone. He's a mercenary. Apparently, he's been coming to Retropolis for some time. Looking for a bigger price."

"I just might have it for him." J mentioned.

Gozen and Firebolt went across the suburb areas of Retropolis and the industrial division of the city. They scouted to find nothing related to Onyx or J. While they scouted, The Swordman met with the Huntswoman in the low sections of Retropolis. The Swordman found her trying to steal some valuable items from an auction that is set to start the following day.

"Knew I'll find you here."

The Huntswoman turned around to see The Swordman

and she only smiled and approached him without any fear.

"You only come to ruin the fun."

"What you're doing is not what I would call fun."

"It's fun for me. Maybe not for you because of all your morals."

"I came here to ask you of something. Something that is important."

'How important is this that you're asking of me? Is it something of a global threat like the ones you were in when those things came from the sky?"

"It is not global. It's urban. The city is about to be hit with a turf war between Onyx and J and I will need your help in stopping it from increasing further out into other areas."

"Why not let them settle it. I mean, if one kills the other, isn't that much better. You know, one gone and only one more left."

"If it comes to that, then that is what it will be. For right now, it is up to us to stop them both before the crossfire reaches those that are not a part of their war."

"Let me think on it."

The Swordman turned, continuing to speak to Huntswoman.

"If I find you out in this area again, I will have to stop you with force."

"You could've stopped me with force right now, but you didn't, and I know why. You don't have to explain anything of it to me. I already know enough."

"I'm sure that you do."

Back at Sir Onyx's hideout, he stood before his gang and declared the war against J. By making the announcement. Onyx revealed who he has chosen to stand by his side. The man walked up toward Onyx and the gang. Dressed in a dark gray and black stealth attire, wearing a gray mask with scopes on the eyes. On his sides are several handguns and on his back is a rifle.

"This man right here is known in our circle as Gunbaine. I have chosen him as my right-hand man. As of this moment, his first order of business is to assassinate Conley. By any means possible."

Meanwhile, at J's hideout, the gang is there and they're cheering on J's name. J enters the warehouse room and showcasing to them his chosen man for the war. The man entered the room, dressed in military gear colored in dark blue and gray. His eyes were red from the stealth helmet and mask he wore, and he carried with him an arsenal of weapons. Including a sword of his own.

"I have chosen this man right here to assist me in this war against Sir Onyx. Maveth, the Death-Bringer. He will put an end to Sir Onyx with his skills. That I know he can accomplish."

III

<u>CROSSFIRE</u>

Sir Onyx and J have begun their war in Retropolis. The downtown streets are filled with gunshots and violence. Civilians have been urged to avoid the downtown area by any means. Due to the increase of chaos, Mayor Charles Baker has declared to close the downtown area until the turf war between Onyx and J has been complete. However, the Retropolis Police Department head out to the downtown area.

"What's the plan?" Detective Justine Copeland asked.

"We put a stop to this nonsense." Commissioner Austin replied. "Save this city once more."

"Hey, Commissioner." Detective Cash Hankinson said. "What about what the Mayor had said earlier in the office? About the city being at risk of martial law?"

"Now isn't he time to discuss the matter."

Throughout the ongoing gang shootout, Gunbaine and Maveth stood nearby on the opposing sides. Maveth savored the sounds of the gunfire. Gunbaine prepared himself, grabbing his rifle.

"I need to get on top of that building."

"By all means." Onyx said. "Make sure you hit Conley. Hit him good."

"My pleasure."

Gunbaine made his move to reach higher ground. Maveth grabbed his sword, turning toward J.

"If you please, I can wipe out all his men in a single stroke."

"How can you do that?" J asked. "You have super-speed or something?"

"Something of the sort. It's your call."

J nodded. He looked at Maveth, who gripped his sword and held his left hand on his gun.

"Go for it." J said.

Maveth moved with haste, running into the middle of the shootout. J stopped his men from firing as Maveth ran through Onyx's gang. Blocking their shots with his sword and firing back. Those closer to him were slashed by his sword as he dodged and swiped at others nearby. Onyx watched as his men were being taken out by Maveth.

"The hell is this guy?" Onyx wondered.

On the rooftop, Gunbaine looked, seeing Maveth's damage to Onyx's men.

"Well, well. If it isn't old Danton Thomas. Funny how things work out."

Onyx's gang is dead. Their blood flowed through the area. Onyx backed up as Maveth approached him. Holding his sword in front. J and his men followed Maveth, J stepped in between Onyx and Maveth.

"Where the hell did you find him?!" Onyx yelled.

"I have my sources, Fargo. Fitting, where's your special guy?"

"Oh, he's here. In the right spot for the kill."

Maveth looked around and gazed up, catching a familiar glare. He stared toward a rooftop, seeing Gunbaine and his rifle ready.

"Smalls."

Maveth ran for the building with J looking at him.

"Where are you going?"

"To take out Onyx's little helper!" Maveth said. "Do what you will with him. I will handle this guy myself."

"Noted." J said.

Maveth made it up to the rooftop, finding himself faced with a gun. Gunbaine laughed as he aimed it steady toward the Death-Bringer.

"Crazy how life works out, huh." Gunbaine said.

"It is such." Maveth replied. "You were always around to take my job."

"I go wherever the money whispers. You know this."

"I know it more than others. Why align yourself with Onyx? What did he promise you?"

"He promised me money. A lot of money. Plenty enough to make my ideas come to pass."

"Is working with A.B. and her little Enforcement Order part of the ideas?"

"How do you know about that?"

"My ears are within all secret places. Keeps me focused on the grand prize."

"So, J promised to deliver you the prize. Millions of cash?"

"He promised me gold, silver, and some copper. It'll get the job done and the improvements will come as planned."

"Then, what stops me from shooting you?"

"Nothing. Only the fact you'll be wasting your bullets as I slash your throat. Your blood will pour down this building for Onyx to see and then, J will kill him. Claiming the criminal underworld as his own. Simple choices at play."

Police sirens echoed through the area as Austin, Justine, and Cash arrived at the scene. They jumped out of the car, aiming their guns toward the two crime lords and J's men. Seeing the bodies of Onyx's gang on the ground gave them a cause for concern.

"Your men do this, J?" Austin asked.

"Just one man."

Maveth and Gunbaine looked down, seeing the police.

"This isn't what I signed up for." Gunbaine said. "This was supposed to be a clean kill."

"You're afraid of the cops?"

"No."

"Then, what's stopping you from getting paid?"

Gunbaine chuckled under his mask.

"You were always the one with words, Danton."

Gunbaine aimed his rifle. Steady. Steady. One shot. The shot fired, hitting the police car. Justine and Cash began firing toward the roof with Austin moving for a position. Onyx and J moved to another area. Maveth and Gunbaine ducked on the rooftop.

"You should've hit them." Maveth said.

"All part of the plan, big man."

Engine sounds roared near the scene as Onyx and J noted the Land-Dagger arriving. Maveth and Gunbaine also could see the car from below. The cockpit opened as The Swordman jumped out with Gozen and Firebolt at his side.

"Ah shit!" Gunbaine said. "He's here."

"Yes." Maveth said calmly. "He is."

J's men ran toward them, entering a fight. Gozen and Firebolt took them out without hesitation. The Swordman stared at the two crime lords and gazed over to Austin.

"Get yourselves out of here!" The Swordman yelled.

"Is he telling us to leave?" Justine asked.

"Go now!" The Swordman yelled once more. "We will handle this situation."

"Best we do as the man says!" Cash said, running to the police car.

Justine and Cash entered the car with Austin approaching Swordman. Gozen and Firebolt stood by his side. Austin gave them a nod as he entered the car, driving off. The Swordman focused his attention on Onyx and J.

"This turf war is over!"

"Is it?" J said. "What do you think, Fargo?"

"Maybe it's just begun."

Gunbaine fired another shot, hitting the ground where The Swordman stood. He looked up to see both Gunbaine and Maveth. He turned to Gozen and Firebolt quickly.

"You tow, keep Onyx and J from doing any more harm."

"Where are you going?" Gozen asked.

"To meet the two on the rooftop."

The Swordman grappled himself, moving upward to the roof. His feet touch the rooftop and he stared down Gunbaine and Maveth. Neither man made a move. Only the eyes were locked on. Weapons were in hand. The rooftop quickly became a calm place within the shootout.

"Blake Smalls." The Swordman said.

"You know my name? Nice."

The Swordman looked over to Maveth. He remembered something as Maveth raised his sword, pointing it toward him.

"That night." The Swordman said. "You remember?"

"I do." Maveth said. "I've waited for this moment. The chance to take you out is a grand prize above all others."

The Swordman reached, pulling out his sword and pointing it toward Maveth and Gunbaine.

"Then, this is your chance to claim that prize."

"Will do!" Maveth yelled as he and The Swordman clashed.

IV

<u>GAME OF WAR</u>

The Swordman and Maveth had themselves a clashing of swords. Twists and turns between the two men. Gunbaine managed himself to get a perfect aim at The Swordman during his fight.

"Just stay still for a second." Gunbaine whispered. "Stay… still."

Gunbaine took the shot and Maveth's sword blocked the bullet from hitting The Swordman. Maveth shoved Swordman and turned toward Gunbaine, twisting his sword in hand.

"Why did you foil the shot?" Gunbaine asked.

"The Swordman is mine." Maveth declared. "I've been waiting for this prize for a while. I will not allow your actions to ruin it for me."

The Swordman moved like a quickening shadow, attacking Maveth from the side and kicking Gunbaine to the ground of the rooftop. Maveth rose up, tossing kicks and punches toward the Swordman. Swordman blocked the maneuvers as quickly as he possibly could. Maveth drove his sword forward, causing The Swordman to grab it, snatching it from his hands. The Swordman used the end of Maveth's sword to smack him in the face before swiping

Maveth's chest with his own blade. Gunbaine raised up his arm-pistols and The Swordman tossed Maveth's sword toward him, slicing the pistol muzzle.

"Shit!" Gunbaine yelled.

Gunbaine looked at his forearm, seeing the damaged muzzle. He looked up and The Swordman pounced onto him like an animal hunting. Maveth watched as The Swordman took out Gunbaine. Afterwards, The Swordman and Maveth stood still, looking at one another. The Swordman grabbed Maveth's sword from the ground and tossed it to him.

"I prefer fair fights."

"Good." Maveth said. "Next time then."

Maveth dropped a smoke grenade to the ground. The Swordman ran into the blast and all he could see as the smoke moved through the air was no one. As the smoke cleared for his view, he realized both Maveth and Gunbaine were gone. Looking around, he didn't see them near the rooftop.

"Damn." The Swordman uttered.

Swordman dropped to the streets, only to see both Onyx and J being taken into custody by Commissioner Austin and his detectives. Austin approached the Swordman with a certain ease. Looking over to the crime lords in the truck.

"Your allies did a work on them."

"They're trained for such an occasion."

"Thank you for helping Retropolis once more."

"It's why I'm here."

The Swordman left with Gozen and Firebolt from the scene.

Days later, news broke out of Onyx and J being locked

in Rockward Penitentiary. Gozen and Firebolt have declared to remain in Retropolis to help with further causes and to evade potential threats from all corners. In the outskirts of Retropolis, Maveth stood. His helmet off as he smirked overlooking the city and its reconstruction.

"Next time, *Myth-Walker*. Next time." Maveth said, turning away from Retropolis.

Kenari sat within the Swordlair as Allison herself was training in armed combat on the other end. Kenari was reading up on some strange details of activities caused by Death throughout the world. Knowing she's in Pegasus Prison ever since the Battle of Retropolis. Circumstances did not add up according to his knowledge. However, he recently got his hands on a file from an anonymous source from T.I.T.A.N. the file read of criminals working in a unit.

"*Enforcement Order 66.*" Kenari said.

I

THE OUTBAND

Late during a night near Enigma City, a pair of men in black suits scattered across a building once owned by Kex Kendrick. However, with Kendrick in prison after he events of the Battle of Retropolis, the building was evicted and went up for sale. Now, it has been purchased by an unknown buyer. The men in suits are his associates as they placed strange technology into the building.

"How much does the boss require we pace inside?"

"As much that can fit."

"What is all of this anyway? Anyone know?"

"Boss said to keep things quiet. Otherwise the one above him will make us quiet. I'll rather keep my mouth close than let to flow."

Upon doing so, Taltus The Powerman bolted to the building, seeing the technology. Dark, black, and appearing like onyx with the scent of burnt coal. one of the men looked up, seeing Taltus hovering above them.

"What is all of this?" Taltus asked.

"It's him!" The man yelled.

The suits began shooting at Taltus. The bullets bounced off his white and blue suit as he came down, taking out the guns with his lightning vision. He rallied the men together before having them stand against the wall. In one swoop, he knocked them unconscious with a quick slap to the head. Afterwards, he entered the building, seeing boxes upon boxes of the strange technology, he went through, he found one man working on some of the technology. Hovering toward him, he frightened the man by his appearance.

"Don't harm me!" The man yelled.

"I'm not here to hurt you. I need to know what's all this? This technology doesn't fit the details of human hands."

"Because, it isn't human."

"What is it?"

"It's from the dark ones of the sky."

"Dark ones?"

"Our boss has spoken with him. His arrival is near and this all belongs to him."

"His name. Tell me his name."

"I cannot." The man said. "For he knows me. He sees my every move. If I was to spout out his name, a beam of light will come down and kill me. I cannot for my life's sake."

"Where's your boss?" Taltus asked.

"In Enigma City. On business works."

"I will speak to him myself. Clean this place out before I destroy all that sits in here."

Taltus flew away from the building, heading for Enigma City. The man inside however sighed as a dark mist crouched over him. He felt calm and steady. The mist vanished, following Taltus' trail.

II

FOR YOUR MASTER

Taltus headed toward Enigma City, a beam of light emerged from the ground, striking the Powerman out of the air. Taltus fell to the ground, dragged through the dirt from the impact of the blast. As he stopped, he looked up, finding himself surrounded by trees. Standing up, Taltus walked forward, entering an open field. There, he saw a brute figure. Scruffy hair and dressed in clad armor.

"Why did you do that?" Taltus asked.

"It was the only way to gain your attention."

"Who are you?"

"Dominix. I come from another dimension far from this world. Far from Olympus."

"Zeus sent you?"

"Zeus is not my master. I have been chosen to eliminate you."

"Eliminate me? On what causes?"

"Enough prattle!"

Dominix rushed toward Taltus, ending up being punched across the field. Taltus flew over Dominix's moving body and continued to beat down the dimensional being. Taltus grabbed Dominix by his hair and slammed him into the ground. Dominix paused to catch his breath.

"How are you moving this fast?"

"I've gained much abilities during my lifetime."

"He spoke of such things."

"So spoke?"

"Never mind!" Dominix yelled. "I will kill you and feed your corpse to the hounds of Blachole!"

Dominix lunged with his fist in front. Taltus grabbed a hold of his arm and tossed him once again, this time near a set of trees. Dominix crashed through the trees like a falling aircraft. Taltus flew over him, hovering as he watched the brute recover from the impact.

"You've got heart." Taltus said. "I'll give you that."

"Don't accuse me of being soft."

"I'm not. You attacked me first. I'm only returning the favor."

"Fool! I attacked you for a variety of reasons!"

"Then, explain."

"Trespassing in a place you shouldn't belong! Touching such technology you haven't even begun to process. My master knows of your existence. The power you possess. The allies you have made. He is coming. I am only the pure sign of his arrival. My attack was only a prelude of his actions."

"When can I meet your master?"

"He's not on your time. You're on his!"

"I guess I'll have to make him show up."

Taltus speared Dominix, beating him down into the dirt. The impact of Taltus' punches created a crater for Dominix to lay in. After Taltus finished pummeling the brute. A strange and odd portal opened up in front of them both. Here, a large figure walked out. Standing with intent. Purpose. He walked with a class to his character. Walking past Taltus as if he wasn't there. The figure stood over Dominix. Dominix raised his eyes, seeing the figure and immediately bowed in fear.

"Forgive me. I did not know you were coming this day."

"You are to return to Blachole." The figure declared. "Your work requires you elsewhere."

"But, permit me the opportunity to eliminate this titagod. He is standing in your way."

"Leave. I will handle the titagod on my own."

Dominix bowed before entering the opened portal. Taltus watched as the figure turned around, staring at him. Looking deep into his eyes. Taltus did the same. Neither moved an inch.

"Who are you?" Taltus asked.

The figure only grinned as he walked past Taltus once again. Taltus rushed over, placing his hand on the figure's shoulder. The figure turned, backslapping Taltus across the field. Taltus shook his head, rubbing his face. He glared at the class brute.

"You thought that would keep me down?!"

The figure decided to unleash a series of energy beams from his eyes. The impact of the beams on Taltus' body caused him to collapse from the intense heat and the scorching cuts. Taltus fell and the figure stepped forward onto the portal, but turned his head, looking at the downed titagod.

"Remember this moment." The figure said. "Soon, humanity will be in your position. Bowing before *Oranos of Blachole*. The end has come."

Oranos vanished into the portal and was gone. Like a lightning bolt after its strike. Taltus arose to his feet, finding only himself in a large open field.

III

INVASION OF BLACHOLE

The following day, everything was going as usual in Enigma City. Civilians went about their business and there was hardly any crime taking place in the streets ever since Taltus was known to the public, criminals thought twice about taking their actions out in the open. Like a great boom of thunder in the sky, a portal had opened above the city. Its light shining down upon the city like a spotlight had been placed upon the civilians. They gazed up tot eh portal as it roared with a machine-sounding hum. While staring, strange creatures began to pour out of the portal, flying down to the streets, terrorizing anyone who was near their presence.

The creatures had the strange appearance of wolves, but with eagle-like wings and talons. Afterwards, a man-like being hovered down behind them. He carried a large staff, covered in dark-golden armor. His helmet appeared reminiscent of goats. He stepped on the streets, looking at the panicking crowds.

"His is what he desires! For you all to prepare yourselves for his grand return. This is the day of many things to come!"

While he cherished the moment of fainting screams and

gushing sounds, Taltus appeared like a missile out of nowhere, snatching the horned being from the ground and flying up from the city.

"Who are you?" Taltus asked.

"You're him."

"I'm who?"

"The one he confronted."

Taking his staff, he swiped Taltus from him as they both fell to the streets unharmed. Taltus arose from the fall and stared at the being, twirling his staff with a grin on his face.

"Why have you come to this place?"

"Why do you care?"

"It's my duty to protect."

"Duty? Then, you must have some militaristic experience."

"I've had my share in the past."

"Well, this isn't the past. We're in the future."

"If so, how come I don't know your name."

"Forgive my manners. The name is Thrudhawk. The general of Blachole."

"Blachole?" Taltus uttered. "I've heard of the place from a unusual being."

"Have you? My, you've made this encounter much more intriguing to my mind."

Thrudhawk rushed toward Taltus with the staff. Taltus grabbed the staff like a bolt, taking it from the Blacholian general and smashing him with it to the side. Taltus dropped the staff as Thrudhawk extended his right hand. The staff rose up from the ground and flew back to his hand.

"Retracting weapons in your world?" Taltus said.

"We have much more. We desire to share it with this world and humankind. For our pleasure."

"You seek to enslave humanity."

"Fool. They're already enslaved. They just don't know it yet."

Thrudhawk shoved the staff into Taltus' throat and tripped him with it. He stood over the Powerman and started pummeling him with the staff. Taltus used his arms to block the ongoing strikes before focusing his eyes and unleashing his lightning vision, hitting Thrudhawk in the chest, knocking him into the air and back down.

"Ugh. Ophfiends, attack!" Thrudhawk yelled.

The flying wolf-like creatures zoomed toward Taltus in droves. Thrudhawk stepped back and watched as his legion fought against the Powerman. Using their talons, claws, and fangs to attack him at every end. Taltus struggled to get through the flying creatures. Taltus took a second to breath in and as he exhaled, he busted the ophfiends from him. Kicking them around all corners. From there, Taltus grabbed Thrudhawk by his throat and tossed him into a pack of the ophfiends.

"I only have one question." Taltus said, walking over toward Thrudhawk. "Who is Oranos?"

"Why do you seek to know?" Thrudhawk gestured. "What do you think he can do for you?"

"I met him in the fields. He gave me a warning of his coming. He said he was of Blachole. You proclaimed yourself a general of the place."

"Because I am."

"Where is this Blachole?"

"In a place far from this world."

"How far?"

"Very. Only a portal will grant anyone entry into the dark dimension."

"So, you, your army, Dominix, and this Oranos all come from the same place."

"Yes. Oranos has proclaimed this world his to rule. Humanity will bow before him when he returns in full."

"How about I pay him a visit instead."

Taltus dropped Thrudhawk to the ground and pointed in the sky.

"Open the portal. Now."

"I will not!"

Taltus punched Thrudhawk to the point of his helmet cracking above his head.

"Open the portal if you wish to continue breathing!"

Thrudhawk grinned. Nodding his head as he reached toward the gauntlet on his left forearm. He smiled as he pressed a button.

"He said you would be a challenge."

The thunder cracked in the sky and the portal reappeared. Opened brightly above them. Taltus looked up toward it. Certain.

"I'm entering your realm. When I return and if I see you still here, I will kill you and your entire army."

Thrudhawk laughed. The ophfiends flew into the portal, leaving the city with Thrudhawk hovering with them.

"Enter Blachole, titagod! Oranos is waiting for you."

They became one with the portal's light, Taltus bolted from the ground and into the portal. Last thing he saw was the flash of light, leaving this world and entering another.

IV

<u>LEGACY</u>

Taltus moved in a clear and still atmosphere. He couldn't glimpse at what was around him. For there was only darkness and darkness remained. The air was silent and cold. Taltus continued moving forward trough the dark before seeing a glint of light ahead. He pushed himself further toward the light and was pulled from the darkness. Finding himself in another place. A place of cooling fire and lightning.

"This is Blachole." Taltus said.

He flew over the bridge from the entrance toward a giant castle. Made of darkened stones and flowing with cosmic energy. In the air, Taltus saw more ophfiends, going to and fro. They didn't bother to harm him in any way, which caught him by surprise. Flying closer to the castle doors, they opened. Stopping him as he landed to his feet and walked in. In the castle, Taltus found himself staring at Thrudhawk leaning against the stone wall. Tending to his wounds. He even saw Dominix standing before him near a throne. At the throne, Oranos sat with a smile on his face.

"There you are." Taltus said.

"You came." Oranos said.

"I figured I would. Come see what this place was all

about."

"And what do you think of it?"

"Too dark for my taste. Some sunlight would make this place better."

"There is no sun in this dimension, titagod. For where you stand doesn't operate as the earth. You've entered an ancient place. One made up of a divine hand."

"Funny. The gods of Olympus would say the same about their mountain. What is it with all these dimensions and all these rulers? Who has the final say above all things?"

"Even though you are an impressive specimen of a newly species, such knowledge would crush your intellect to know the truth."

"I came here only to learn one thing. Why attack the earth? Why humanity?"

"It is my will. The earth has been in the dominion of humanity for a long time. Many have ruled it in the past. From dark gods to cosmics to the divine forces above. But, I have yet to receive my opportunity at the chance. Now, it is my time."

"And you've chosen to give those of evil your technology? To use in your will?"

"The Outband summoned me with an ancient sacrifice. I answered their petition and granted them such equipment. With it, they will slowly enslave the human population all in my name. They will bear my mark and they will worship me above all their gods."

"Not if I have a say in the matter."

"I saw your actions when those dark forces came from the sky in that city you call Retropolis. Your unfenced with the others. Forming yourselves into a team. How, you have shown us a lot about your skill set."

"Things have changed for the better I will believe."

"They will once I have dominion over the earth."

"I'll kill you before you make the move."

"Will you?" Oranos said. "You defeated my son, Dominix. Took down Thrudhawk, my general. You really believe you can defy and kill Oranos of Blachole?"

"I know I can."

"Hmm." Oranos said. "I will not make a fool out of you just yet. For I do not wish to have titagod blood stain my floors and castle."

"You will have no choice."

"Better prepare yourselves and warn your allies of my coming. For it is soon and it is Oranos' will."

Taltus flew toward Oranos with his fist in front. Preparing to strike. Oranos raised his right hand slowly and froze Taltus in place in the air.

"Such anger flows through him. His future is clear, bur vaigely shadowed by himself. It is done."

Oranos pushed his hand forward, shoving Taltus from the castle and back to the entrance, where the portal had opened. Taltus entered the portal and within that second, he was out of Blachole.

Taltus fell from the portal over Enigma City. Falling, his eyes opened, catching himself and he flew from the city, returning to the Fortress of Cytron to recover.

Afterwards, the Enigma City news discussed the strange portals in the air, leading the city to believe aliens were invading. Stephanie Vale and Alex Havens set themselves aside to uncover more about the portals as they went out to meet with the Powerman.

THE NANO MAN: NANOTECH DEBATE

I

<u>CONSEQUENCES ABORT</u>

Nathan Hawke traveled from Newark, New Jersey to Washington D.C. after receiving notice of the U.S. Senate desiring to speak to him concerning his Nano Man technology. His involvement of the exposits have triggered the minds of the political parties and Hawke has set to speak with them. To give them understanding of the Nano Man and his purpose.

Entering the U.S. Capital Building, Hawke is amazed to find President Donald Trump sitting. Trump's eyes caught Hawke as he entered. Trump waved and Hawke waved back. Both are business partners in a series of firms. Some public, others secret. As Hawke sat down, Rick Carter entered, sitting next to Hawke.

"Didn't know you would be here." Hawke said.

"I had no choice but to come. Otherwise, this whole thing could blow out of proportions."

"Oh, come on."

"Out of everyone in this place, I know how you can be when someone is after your work."

Hawke nodded.

"Hmm, you really do." Hawke smirked. "Where's Alice? She here too?"

"I would assume so."

"That's great. This can be a party now instead of a bummer-fest."

"Just don't do anything rational."

"Trust me. I won't. But, them, I can't speak for."

"I understand."

Crowds filled the seats of the Capital Building as the Senate were preparing to speak, Trump intervened, grabbing the microphone.

"Excuse me, everyone." Trump said. "But, I feel it is for the better that I speak with Mr. Hawke concerning the Nano Man technology."

"I agree." Hawke replied. "He knows me."

Hawke looked over to Rick, who could only stare at his friend. Hawke smiled back.

"He knows me." Hawke said.

"I know already." Rick replied with a still face.

"Now, I do not know as much as some of you may say. But, Nathan Hawke, is a true friend." Trump said. "An honest one. One that I believe if he had something that could change America for the better, he would be the one to tell us himself."

"That I would." Hawke smiled.

"Nathan, would you go ahead and tell the Senate and me all there is to know about this Nano Man technology."

"Sure thing, Mr. President."

Nathan sat up in his seat, looking at Trump and the Senate. He nodded.

"The Nano Man technology is in good hands. There is not viable danger ahead. I know you're all aware of the events in Newark with the Geier and the religious fanatics. You're also aware of the happening in Canada where The

Nano Man assisted many others like himself to save the world, mind you from an inter-dimensional threat."

"That's not why we're here, Nathan." Trump said. "We need to know about the technology. Not what he has achieved with such capability. I'm not Obama. His Administration ended when I entered the White House. So, do not tell us about his actions in aiding a foreign country."

"Then, what do you want with the tech? Tell me?"

"The tech should belong to the United States Military. The Army, the Navy, the Air-Force, the Marines and the Space Force should have full access to that kind of weaponry."

"They have tech that is beyond the Nano Man's own exosuit."

"Are you telling us the truth, Mr. Hawke?" A Senator asked.

"I'm telling you what I know. That's all I can tell you. I can lie, truthfully. But, that is not why I'm here. You called me and I am here to tell you there's no immediate danger."

"What if Iran got a hold of the tech?" Trump asked. "Would you take responsibility for that?"

"How would Iran gain the Nano Man tech in the first place? There's no Iranian threat coming my direction. Why would there be?"

"What about China?" Trump asked. "Have you considered them and the fact the trade deals are a bust?"

"I didn't know this was about trade. Are we entering another trade war or something?"

"You've looked at all possibilities?"

"Every last one." Hawke said. "It's my duty to make sure nothing happens with the Nano Man technology. If something was to take place, it would be on my hands and my conscious alone.”

“Nathan.” Trump said. “It would be for the best you deliver all the Nano Man technology to us immediately.”

“And what if I choose otherwise?”

“Don’t tempt us.” A Senator said. “We have ways of doing such.”

“Oh, I know.” Hawke grinned. “I’m not going to turn it over though.”

Trump sighed. Looking around at the Senate. Pointing at Hawke. The Senate said words toward Trump. Hawke looked over to Rick.

“They’re going to take the tech, Nate.”

“We’ll see.”

Trump nodded, turning back to Hawke.

“You have twenty-four hours to hand over the Nano Man technology or face dire consequences.”

“Heh.” Hawke said. “Like fire and fury?”

“Turn it over.” Trump declared. “Save yourself the trouble of facing your country.”

“I’m not turning it over. Everything is smooth. No problems at all. Yet, you’re looking to cause a problem. Out of all the things happening in the world right now, you’re looking to start an internal war between the government and a fellow citizen?”

“America First.” Trump said. “Remember that.”

Trump left the panel as the Senate demanded Hawke turn over the Nano Man technology. Hawke stood up and left the room. Rick followed him to the outside as he walked toward his car.

“I’m going to head over to the bunker before they do.”

“Why?”

“Because, I believe they’ve already sent out a squad to

take the tech."

Hawke sighed.

"If you see them, do whatever it takes to stop them."

"I'm not taking out my own countrymen."

"Your countrymen over your friend?"

"That's not what I meant."

"We'll see."

Rick returned to the bunker. Taking out his phone.

"Nate. It's gone. Most of it is gone. I'm sorry, man."

Hawke listened and kept quiet.

"I'll take care of it." Hawke said.

"Don't do anything stupid, alright. We'll get to the bottom of this."

"Yeah. We will."

Hawke ended the call and sighed. Knowing now he's going to enter a war with his own country. Something he hoped to avoid. He looked at his phone, dialing Alice's number.

II

<u>NANOTECH IN GETTYSBURG</u>

Nathan sat in the Nano-Bunker, seeing only a portion of his technology remaining. Alice entered the lair, seeing Nathan distressed. Staring into space with his hands together. She approached him slowly. He quickly looked over to see her.

"Didn't hear you come in."

"I had to come. Rick told me of the news. I'm sorry I didn't attend the meeting."

"It wasn't big of a deal. Just a bunch of political puppets. That's all."

"And what of your tech?"

"I'm going to get it back."

"Get it back? How?"

"Like I've done with most oppositions in my way. Take them out."

"Nate, this is the United States Government you're talking about. You can't just take them out."

Nathan stood up from his seat and walked over to the closet, gazing at Alice.

"I can."

Nathan grabbed the object in the closet and left the bunker.

Within another undisclosed location, President Trump met with Chance Parker, a competitor to Nathan Hawke, CEO of ParkerTech. The two sat down at a table while the Secret Service kept guard at the doors and windows. Parker rubbed his tan slim suit. Checking his black tie, making sure it's on properly. He's overly concerned with looking good. Shaking hands as they sat down.

"I have to thank you, Mr. President for contacting me. I never imagine what would be happening right now."

"You know why we're having this meeting. Nathan Hawke is treading the water of America. His actions will get him killed."

"I know that. It's Hawke's nature to test the ground he walks on. Besides, I'm a better guy when it comes to such technology. I mean, I am his competition after all."

"And you have similar technology to the Nano Man?"

"Something of the sort, it isn't quite ready for commission yet. Still some bugs we have to work through."

"How about what you have now?"

"What I have now?"

"Yes. What would be your plan, if you were in my position to stop Hawke from causing further harm to himself and to this country?"

"Well, I would assassinate him."

"Assassinate him?" Trump questioned. "How come?"

"Rid myself of the competition. But, I wouldn't be the one to make the mark."

"You're talking as if you've planned this."

"Oh, I've planned a lot of things. But, taking Hawke out is only a small fraction of the plans. However, I know a guy who can handle Hawke while you and your Administration deal with the nanotech."

"Is he an American?"

"No doubt. Wouldn't hire anyone else to do the job. He's good. I can assure you of that."

"How soon can he be ready?" Trump asked.

"He's already prepared." Parker said. "Just say the word."

Trump nodded. Standing up from the chair. Extending his hand. Parker stood up and shook the President's hand. Trump grinned.

"Make the call, Parker. Get him on the job immediately."

"Will do, Mr. President."

Later in the day, Parker returned to his headquarters and inside was a peculiar man, standing at his desk. Overlooking the diagram of armored exosuits. The man wore red and black armor and carried a scarred mask with him. Parker shut the office door, getting the man's attention.

"You made it over here quickly." Parker said.

"As soon as you made the call, I was on my way." The man said, turning around.

"I like that. Disciplined." Parker gestured, walking over to his chair. "You know why I called you here?"

"You want me to do the task. Find Hawke and take him out."

"Absolutely. But, do it discreetly. Clean kill. No slashing or gushing of blood. We can't have that at this moment. Too many eyes on Hawke."

"I'll get the job done. I expect to be paid as soon as it's done."

"You will be. Trust me."

"I don't trust anyone wearing a suit and sitting in an office."

"Then, you're already on the mark."

On the TV in the office, the news broadcasted a sighting of the Nano Man hovering over the Gettysburg Battlefield. Parker's eyes went big as the man he hired left the office. Parker watched the screen as Nano Man just hovered still, overlooking the field.

"The hell is he up to?"

The news spread of Nano Man in Gettysburg across the country. President Trump wasn't having it and immediately assigned the United States Army to infiltrate the battlefield to take down Nano Man by any means. The Army went out in tanks, jeeps, and footmen. Trump watched from the Oval Office as the event was being broadcasted on Fox News. CNN and MSNBC refused to show details regarding the Nano Man's purpose in the field. Claiming it to be a protest against the Trump Administration. Crowds gathered near the Gettysburg Battlefield to watch the confrontation.

Alice and Rick watched from the Hawke Industries headquarters. Both were unaware of Nathan's plans to travel to Gettysburg.

On the battlefield, a soldier stepped out of the jeep, looking up at the Nano Man. Holding a bullhorn.

"You have ten seconds to come down and surrender the armor."

"Ten seconds?" Nano Man said. "That's all you're giving me."

"Ten!"

"Nine."

"Eight."

"Seven."

"Six."

"Come on!" Nano Man said. "Hurry it up, will you."

"Five!"

"Four!"

"Three!"

"Two!"

"One!" The soldier turned back, entering his jeep. "Fire at will!"

The footmen began firing their rounds toward Nano Man, who flew and swooped around the gunfire. He held his wrists out, firing a blast of energy, knocking down the foot soldiers with a bit of ease. He stopped and gestured toward the tanks and jeeps.

"Where's your real firepower?" Nano Man asked. "I demand you use it if you're going to take this tech from me!"

The tanks began firing the cannons toward Nano Man. Moving swiftly from the blast, he fired another set of energy beams from both wrists, burning up the tanks as the soldiers bolted out of the vehicle. Flying over them and repeating the same action, soldiers only stood by and watched as Nano Man took out their jeeps and tanks in a quick succession. Trump watched the event as it happened and shook his head.

"I don't like this. Get Parker on the phone now."

"Yes, Mr. President."

"I can't believe this." Trump said.

Burned jeeps and tanks covered the field. Nano Man

looked over toward Sherfy farm, seeing three tanks approaching. He sighed. Flying over toward them and blasting them with nano-laced missiles from his forearm. The missiles attached themselves to the tanks and shut down their interior system. Causing them to become completely useless.

"Civil War modernized." Nano Man said, overlooking the field.

While most of the country was focused on Nano Man facing the Army at Gettysburg, Geier had returned and quickly attacked the New York/New Jersey areas. Harming civilians and terrorizing them. Geier left the area, flying away before sightings could break out.

Trump grabbed the phone inside the Oval Office. Sitting down with a straight face.

"Parker." Trump said. "You saw the news. Get your guy on the job now."

"He's already on the job, Mr. President." Parker replied. "He'll handle it quickly as possible."

Trump hanged up the phone and turned to the Secretary of State.

"Prepare the Navy, the Air Force, and the Marines. Keep track of Hawke and his every movement. We need to stop him now before his heroic friends get the idea of assisting him."

"Sir, the New York/New Jersey area was attacked by the Geier."

"The birdman who attacked Newark a few months ago?"

"Yes sir."

"Send word out to find him." Trump said. "Any way you can."

“Yes, Mr. President.”

III

<u>BATTLE OF PEARL HARBOR</u>

Walking on the burnt and filled field of the Gettysburg Battlefield, Parker's mercenary walked across the land. Seeing the jeeps, tanks, and injured soldiers. He spotted something glowing on the ground and reached down toward it. He held the small metallic object in his hand and grinned.

"Getting sloppy."

Trump sat in the Oval Office, thinking. A secretary entered the office with Trump giving her a look out of the corner of his eye.

"What do you have for me?" trump said.

"We know where Hawke's next move is."

"And?"

"He's headed for Pearl Harbor."

Trump nodded, looking at an image of Nano Man flying in the air. Trump handed the image back to the secretary.

"Send word out to the Navy. Tell them to take him down by any means."

"Yes sir."

Geier's attack is now traveling across the news in the New York/New Jersey region. Rick and Alice watched the footage on the news. The reporter stated the Geier chose to attack as the debate with Hawke and the U.S. Government has been the talk of the time.

"He decided to do this now." Rick said. "He somehow knew Nate wouldn't be in the area to stop him."

"And Nate won't have any time to stop him. What of the government?"

"They're still on Nate's trail. This Geier attack isn't even on their radar. Much less a concern."

"As long as the Nano Man is out of the public eye, Geier will continue his attacks. There has to be someone we can contact to stop him."

"Who do you have in mind?"

"We could try and call The Powerman guy or The Swordman."

"Too risky." Rick stated. "I have an idea."

"What are you going to do?"

"Put a stop to Geier and save Nate the trouble."

Rick left the room and as he walked, his phone rang. Grabbing it from his pocket, he read the ID and answered quickly.

"Great time, man."

"Yeah. Sorry. I would've one so sooner." Nate said on the other end. "But, being chased can move you a few rounds."

"I see. Where are you?"

"On my way to Pearl Harbor. Figured I could lure Trump's goons out there for another scuffle. You've seen what happened at Gettysburg?"

"We got the news. Listen, Nate, if you don't stop, they

will put you down."

"How good is that going at the moment?"

"Don't doubt their firepower."

"I'm not. I know their firepower."

"That's not the issue."

"And what's the status with you guys?"

"Geier is back."

"Do tell."

"Don't worry about him. I'll take care of it."

"You're going to do it?"

"I have no other choice."

"About time, old friend." Nate said. "Make sure it works properly. Don't want yourself to crash across the skies."

"I think I have it covered."

"Got to go. Tell Alice I'll be back soon."

"Will do."

Hanging up, Rick entered a secure place in the Hawke Headquarters building. Within the room, Rick placed his hand on a scanner, opening a small closet. Within the closet was a silver/chrome exosuit similar to Hawke's but detailed with an arsenal of weaponry. On the suit's chest was a white eagle. Rick smirked.

"Son of a gun."

Rick entered the suit and flew from the facility. Many thought it was Nano Man, but Alice knew who is was and couldn't wrap her head around it.

Arriving at Pearl Harbor, Nathan found the place surrounded with the U.S. Navy. He laughed as he flew around the ships, grabbing everyone's attention and focus.

"I'm here. Aren't you all going to stop me?"

From the grounds came the Admiral. He looked up toward Nano Man and raised his bullhorn.

"You are trespassing on United States Government property."

"That's why I'm here."

"By the orders of President Donald Trump, we are charged with taking you out of the sky."

"What are you waiting for? Shoot me out of the sky, boys!"

The Navy began firing cannons toward Nano Man and he flew through the blasts, rushing toward the weaponized ships. Blasting them into flames with his energy beams. Circling around and shooting the beams, burning anything firing back. The Admiral stood still, watching as the ships were being destroyed in a very quick manner. after the shooting, Nano Man landed in front of the Admiral.

"I tried to tell them." Nano Man said. "The tech is in good hands. Send word to the President. Let him know of this event. I want him to keep coming."

Taking off into the sky, the Nano Man was gone.

In the region of Newark, Geier returned, seeking to terrifying the city once more. As he proceeded, Rick arrived from the sky, landing in the streets for Geier to see. He looked and stared.

"You're not him." Geier said. "Too bulky."

"I'm not the Nano Man. True."

"Then, who are you, imposter?"

"The Silver Eagle."

IV

<u>AIMED IN THE SKY</u>

Nathan decided to return to Newark. Flying in the sky above a large field. He moved still and without notice, a blast occurred, shooting him from the sky and crashing into the field. Upon getting himself in motion. He looked around the area and only saw one individual. The individual was Parker's mercenary. Standing still with a rocket launcher in his hands.

"Who the hell are you supposed to be?" Nano Man asked.

"I'm the guy who will be taking you to meet the President. Paid in full of course."

"You're a mercenary?"

"Yes. The name's Crossface."

"I can only wonder why."

"I'll give you the details once I'm paid and President Trump has you in custody."

"I'm not going into custody. I am not a criminal."

"But you are. You ran off with tech that the government should possess. You attacked the Army at Gettysburg and invaded Pearl Harbor against the Navy."

"How do you know about all of this?"

"I've been tracking you down the moment I was

assigned to find you. It's part of my skill set. Plus, Chance Parker's price was one I couldn't refuse."

"Parker, huh. What did he tell you about facing someone like me?"

"You're no different. If it were so, I would be taking down Enigma City's fellow hero. But, that's not my duty. Yet."

"Looks like I'm going to have to cut your job short."

"I give you the pleasure of trying."

Nano Man blasted an energy beam toward Crossface, who jumped from the attack and fired another blast from the launcher, striking Nano Man. He bounced off the ground from the impact with Crossface reloading as quickly as possible. Nano Man raised up, shaking his head.

"I'm not like the others, Techhead. I'm a whole different kind of deal."

Nano Man blasted another energy bean from his left hand, striking the launcher from Crossface's hands. Crossface turned and quickly, Nano Man speared him to the ground, holding him down.

"Don't try to fight."

"I never give up."

Crossface placed an object on Nano Man's back and in seconds, it exploded. Pushing him from Crossface.

"I am complete with weaponry. I know how this game works."

"So do I."

Nano Man hovered up and blasted Crossface in the legs before grabbing him by his chest and slamming him into the ground. Placing his foot on Crossface's chest and removing his mask to reveal his roughed-up and scarred face.

"Now I see why you're called Crossface."

Nano Man gazed up in the air, seeing something flying toward the area. He looked closer as the figure landed. Crossface also saw the figure.

"The hell is that?" He wondered.

The figure landed in front of the two. Nano Man removed his foot from Crossface and approached the figure who was Rick himself.

"Looks nice on you."

"Don't start." Rick said, wearing the Silver Eagle exosuit.

"Why are you out here?"

"I tracked your suit' movements. Found you here with this guy it seems."

"He's a mercenary. Hired by Change Parker."

"Really? Parker's involved in all of this?"

"What did you expect? Trump assigned him to do it. Had to."

The rushing sounds began to carry in the sky as the U.S. Air Force arrived at the field. Sitting above Nano Man and Silver Eagle. Crossface stayed down, but, crawled from the area. Nano Man saw him and blasted him with a electric net.

"You're not going anywhere."

The Air Force demanded for Nano Man to return with them to D.C. to meet with President Trump. He refused, Rick stood by his friend. The Air Force decided to retaliate, they began firing all rounds toward the two-armed allies. Dodging the attacks, Crossface moved himself further away from the firing field. Nano Man and Silver Eagle combined took down the jets and helicopter of the Air Force. After the flames covered the ground and downed soldiers were scattered across the field, Nano Man turned to Eagle.

"What happened with Geier?"

"I fought against him while you were away. Testing out the suit."

"Is he behind bars once more?"

"No. he escaped. Promised to return only if you were to stop him."

"Then, I know what I must do."

"And that is?"

"Return to Newark and take Geier down. In front of everyone. That way, Trump will understand the Nano Man technology is safer in my hands and not in the possession of the government."

"I will take your word for it."

Hawke glanced at the soldiers and Crossface on the ground.

"What are we going to do about these guys?"

"I'll call it in. bring some assistance." Rick said. "Go to Newark, take down Geier and end all of this before it escalades into a worldwide event."

"Now you're talking."

Nano Man took off while Silver Eagle helped those who were stranded on the field.

V

TRUTH TO POWER

The Nano Man made his return to Newark and once he returned, the Geier appeared before him. Both hovered in the air within the city. Civilians came out to watch as well as the news. Signaling the events across the country. Every news feed gained word of Nano Man's arrival and broadcasted. Trump watched the event from the Oval Office with Parker sitting by.

"What is going on here?" Trump asked. "He ruins Gettysburg, attacks Pearl Harbor and the Navy, and eliminates a portion of the Air Force!"

"I… I don't know." Parker said. "I'm not sure how he's doing it."

"What of your guy? The mercenary. What have you heard from him lately?"

"Nothing yet. But, I know he'll get the job done."

"Then, why hasn't he?"

Parker gulped.

"I will look into it, sir."

Nano Man and Geier continued their stare down.

"I'm surprised you chose to come back."

"Figured I would have to. Heard what you were doing while I was away. Not a good thing, friend."

"With you out of the way, I can create more terror in this place. Now, you have given me what I want."

"My friend told me all about it. Don't worry, you'll be in prison again soon."

"You'll have to kill me before I surrender."

"Don't wish for things you truly don't want."

Geier rushed against Nano Man, striking him with his wings. Nano Man turned around in the air, grabbing Geier's left wing, throwing him to the streets. Civilians moved out of the fight's way as the two began taking punches. Nano Man kicked Geier and slammed him in the chest before ripping off his right wing. The news continued their live feed as the Nano Man stomped on Geier's back.

"This is too easy." He said. "Why are you making this easy for me?"

"I am not giving up!"

"Too late." Nano Man said, ripping off the other wing. "It is done."

Nano Man looked around, finding the news crew. He approached them and stood in the direction of the camera. Looking right into it.

"I want everyone to know. This technology is safe. There is no danger while it rests in my hands. Trust my words or else become like Geier."

The civilians cheered Nano Man's victory. Back at the Oval Office, Trump held his head down, turning off the TV. Parker sat quietly.

"I'll be leaving now." Parker said, leaving the office.

Once the fighting was over, Trump called off the manhunt for the Nano Man tech. Nathan sat in the nano-bunker with all the stolen equipment returned to him. Rick continued to practice the Silver Eagle suit as it upgraded through various training exercises. Geier was placed in a facility known as Ledger Haven.

The following day, Trump entered the bunker to meet with Nathan. Secret Service waited outside the location.

"I don't know how you managed it. But, I still say it's best for the American military to have the tech."

"I understand your reasoning, Mr. President. But, it's safer with me. Not foreign threat is coming with this tech. it's in good hands."

"See to it that it stays that way. Otherwise, we'll be back."

"And I'll be waiting."

Trump nodded and left the bunker. Alice sat with him as he began working on another exosuit. One he promised would take him further out into space. Hidden away in the bunker was a file. The file detailed all the possible solution for when anyone made the attempt to take the Nano Man technology from him. Nathan had prepared himself for the next phase of an attack.

COMMANDER NORLAND: NEW ALBION

I

<u>ARCTIC FIND</u>

Commander Norland and the Champions made their arrival at T.I.T.A.N. Headquarters. Entering the busy base, Colonel Evan Nader approached them with General Sarge Hunter at his side. Shaking the Commander's hand and saluting the Champions. Showing respect as always within the base. A standard procedure ever since the Battle of Retropolis and the formation of The Resistance. His Champions are still the same team as before. Steve Nixon, Woody Fields/Canadian Hawk, Carl James/American Ray, and Andrea Pierson/Whiplash,

"What's the next mission, Colonel?" Norland asked.

"You and your team will be heading out to Alaska. Our intel has told us of an entity roaming around the Alaskan wilderness. We don't know if it's a man or a nubreed or some strange creature. It requires our attention."

"Does it have a name?"

"They call it the Dark Snowman. Apparently, the natives have warned of the being's existence for years."

"We'll solve this, Colonel." Norland said. "Trust us as always."

"Sarge will handle things from here."

Sarge stepped forward as Nader walked away. Norland nodded his departure.

"The drill is simple. Head out to Alaska, confront this Dark Snowman and stop him by any means. Don't kill him, bring him back here for study and analysis. Professor Flm wishes to learn about the entity."

"We'll be on our way."

Norland and the Champions headed out and left the base. Flying off in the hoverjet toward Alaska. Hours later, they arrived in Alaska, landing at a miniature T.I.T.A.N. base, greeting the agents and the soldiers nearby.

"How far out is this Snowman?" Norland asked.

"We've traced the entity's steps further out into the woods. Almost fifteen miles from the base."

"It's moving closer it seems."

"Then, we go to it." Norland said. "We'll handle this threat and give word afterwards."

"Understood."

Norland turned to his team and nodded.

"Let's go."

Norland and the Champions proceeded forward into the woods. Following the tracks. The first thing that caught their attention were the size of the footprints. Larger than an average human.

"This thing is bigger than expected." Woody said.

"Don't let it scare you off." Norland said. "We're a team. We can handle this kind of threat."

Moving forward, the footprints increased, they found a stash of bushes and branches stacked up near a larger tree. Norland stopped the team, looking around the area.

"Keep your ground. It isn't far."

Norland searched the stash and as they were silent, a large figure bolted out of the tress, rushing toward the team. They moved from the attack and Norland turned around to see the figure. The size of its feet matched the prints. It stood over eight feet tall and its body was covered in ice and snow. The figure roared deeply facing Norland.

"Champions!" Norland yelled. "Attack at all corners!"

They moved to attack the Dark Snowman. Striking the monster at every angel. The Snowman grabbed Carl's triangular shield and froze it solid in his hand. Carl stared.

"The hell?"

The Snowman backhanded Carl to the ground. Norland rushed over, striking the Snowman with his fist. Clashing him with punches and kicks. The Snowman tumbled and grabbed Norland by his hand, pushing him into the ground. Norland held the Snowman's hand in his own, pushing back with full strength. From behind, Andrea came, using her electric whips on the Snowman, wrapping them around his arms and shocking him. Norland turned to Nixon.

"Hit him!"

Nixon rushed over, firing a blast from his launcher. Releasing a blast of smoke that caused the Snowman to collapse. Andrea pulled back her whips and Norland walked over, checking the Snowman's pulse.

"He's out." Norland said. "Contact the agents. Tell them we need a large jeep and some assistance."

"Yes sir." Woody said, returning to the base.

The T.I.T.A.N. agents arrived with a jeep and together they brought the Dark Snowman with them to the base. Placing the Snowman on the hoverjet, Norland and the

Champions made their return to the primary headquarters.

Although, in another country, Sinister Judge watched Norland and his team. Using sorcery to create a visible rift to see across lands. He watched as they entered the hoverjet and took off from the base. Judge nodded. Sitting in his lair with his hood cloaking his face. Only his glowing eyes were visible. His plan was set in motion. As it always is.

II

A NEW ALBION

Norland and the Champions made their return to the main headquarters. Unbeknownst to them, they arrived as the headquarters was under attacked. Norland and his team jumped from the landing hoverjet, running toward the base. Inside, they saw robotic figures. Dressed in dark blue and violet cloaks and tunics.

"The hell are these guys?" Nixon asked.

"Doesn't matter." Norland replied. "Let's take them out."

The Champions worked with their skills to take down two of the droids. Norland rushed toward the remaining one, spearing it to the floor and ripping its head from the body. Silent immediately entered the headquarters as Nader and Sarge arrived at the scene, seeing Norland on his knees above the decapitated droid.

"What happened here?" Norland asked.

Nader turned to Sarge. The monitors began to blink with speed and afterwards a face appeared on the monitors. The face of Sinister Judge.

"I see you've met my droids. For they were only a small test to a greater plan. One that will ensure the future of T.I.T.A.N. will submit to Centronian laws and obey me."

"And what if we choose otherwise?" Sarge said.

"Then you will not live to see the New Albion which I will create. My empire above all others. You have a short time to make a decision. I suggest you do so quickly."

The monitors went black as everyone scattered through the headquarters. Norland arose from the ground and approached Nader and Sarge. The Champions stood behind, assisting anyone who was harmed before their arrival.

"What are these?" Norland asked.

"Come with us." Nader said.

Norland followed Nader and Sarge down the hall.

"That man on the screens." Norland said. "Who is he?"

"He is known as the Sinister Judge." Nader replied. "Ruler of a country called Centro. It's far out in between Russia and Germany. Some have speculated his country isn't even under the European Union."

"And you believe that?"

"Yes. Because Judge isn't the kind of man who submits to the authorities of worldly men. Those droids that came in here are called Judgedroids. His soldiers."

"He doesn't have humans working for him?"

"He sees human soldiers as cannon fodder. Says they're a waste on the battlefield. Prefers robots. Durable. Stronger. Faster. It's Judge's pure interest."

"So, why has he chosen to attack you guys?"

"He demands we work for him. Seeing how our technology far surpasses the general population. Judge wants our tech to increase his own."

"He has weapons?"

"A variety of sorts. Some that the world would call science-fiction."

"Like a death ray?"

Nader turned to Norland with a straight face. Norland knew.

"I'm impressed."

"Don't be. Sooner or later, Judge will make another attack before he shows up here on his own. He likes to wait things out. Let them sear into his opponent's mind before they give up. Afterwards, he judges them and executes them if he pleads it so."

Reaching the end of the hallway, Professor Flm walked out of his office, signaling to Norland. Nader nodded to Flm.

"The Professor is expecting you."

"Keep me informed on Judge's workings."

"Will do, Commander."

Norland approached Flm and the two shook hands before entering Flm's laboratory. Inside, they sat down at the table as some of Flm's electrical technology was sparking in the background.

"You managed to take down the droids?"

"Had no other option. Retaliation was all I could muster up."

"Nader told you all you need to know about Sinister Judge?"

"As much. Is there anything else I should know about this man?"

"Well, there is one thing Nader may not have told you."

"Which is?"

"Judge not only works with technology. He delves into sorcery."

"Sorcery? Like magic?"

"He was born into it. It's his first callings. That's how he conquered Centro an renamed the capital city Judgedath."

"So, he's a conqueror and a sorcerer?"

"Yes."

"How do we stop him?"

"I'm not sure about the others. But, you can stop him."

"With my powers. I see."

"However, do not attack Judge with force. Don't go to him unless it's necessary. Judge is known for playing mind games with his enemies."

"I'm surprised Hawke hasn't encountered this man nor as Kenari."

"Hawke and Judge have a similar understanding when it comes to the technology aspect. Kenari and Judge I'm not sure if they've met."

"Now would be a good time."

"But, this is not their battle. It's yours and your team. Just prepare yourself for any attack he sends this way."

"I will."

Over in Judgedath, Centro, Judge sat in his throne room as the front gates of his palace had opened. A young man entered the palace, approaching the room to stand before Judge's seat. The expression of the man was ambition and anger.

"How does it feel to be free from that prison?" Judge asked.

"It feels great. But, why did you have me set free? Why not anyone else in there?"

"Because I know of the power that lives within you. The power to control the elements of the storm."

"That's the reason I was imprisoned. People were afraid

of my potential."

"I do not fear you."

"Then, why bring me here?"

"I have an offer for you."

"What kind of offer?"

"Stand with me as I prepare to create a new Albion in this world. A new empire. Stronger than all those who have come before. I need a solider in the ranks. Standing before my droids. You, I have chosen to be that man."

"Piquing my interest. What will I have to do?"

"Take some of my droids to the headquarters of T.I.T.A.N. and attack them."

"You're going right after the big guys, huh."

"Once you attack, Commander Norland and his Champions will arrive to face you. Then, all will be certain."

"How so?"

"You will see, if you agree to the terms. You are a free man now, Randy Keith."

"Is there money involved in this?"

"I can arrange such."

Randy nodded.

"Fair enough. I accept the terms."

"Good." Judge said slowly. "Now, I will grant you the judgedroids and send you on your way."

"Understood."

III

JUDGMENT SENTENCED

Hours later, Norland sat with his team inside another room in the T.I.T.A.N. headquarters. Agents walked past the room, unable to hear the discussion taking place.

"I've never heard of Centro." Nixon said.

"Many haven't." Norland replied. "But, we have to be on our guard."

"Aren't we always." Andrea said. "We never miss a beat."

"This guy sent robots to attack the base before we even came back here." Woody said. "What if he does it again? How will be ready for something we can't even see or track?"

"Just have to keep our eyes open. This Judge guy is also a sorcerer. He may conjure up projections to confuse us or even harm us. Either way, we have to be careful. Wherever we go."

Thunder cracked above the base. Norland, his team, Nader, and Sarge moved out and walked outside of the base to see above them a massive lightning storm. Yellow lightning streaking across the skies under the dark clouds above them.

"What is this?" Sarge asked.

“I have no idea.” Nader replied.

“It’s him.” Norland said.

“Judge?”

“Yeah. It has to be.”

From the glowing sky, Randy came down with six judgedroids in his possession. Landing in front of the team. Dressed in a dark blue uniform covering his body. Streaks of lightning surrounded his body.

“I never thought I would live to be here.” Randy said.

“Who are you?” Norland asked.

“Why don’t you ask your boss.” Randy said, pointing at Nader. “He knows who I am.”

“Nader, who is this guy? He’s not Judge.”

“He’s Randy Keith. Possesses the ability of conjuring lightning. Some folks inside nicknamed him Thunderstorm.”

Norland turned back to face Randy. Taking notice of the droids standing with him at his side.

“And why do you have Judge’s droids with you?”

“Because I’m on his payroll. Judge set me free from prison and all I have to do is serve him.”

“You know you don’t serve no man.” Nader said. “I’ve seen your act.”

“Judge isn’t an ordinary man. He’s much more than that. The power he possesses is capable of many things. His new Albion will be one to dwell in.”

“You need to find something else to do.” Sarge uttered. “Instead of sending threats and wasting our time. Much less yours.”

The Champions were prepared for the fight as was Norland. Nader’s hand was set at his side. Sarge had the walkie on standby. Stepping forward, Norland stared at

Randy. Trying to reason with him.

"No need to do this."

"I have no other choice. Besides, I've been wanting to do some damage."

Randy blasted Norland with a lightning bolt. The judgedroids ran toward the Champions. Fighting them. Nader and Sarge raised up their guns, firing at Randy, but with his power, melted the bullets in mid-air. Winking at Nader with a smile on his face. Norland stood up and tackled him. Randy shook his head as he blasted Norland with another lightning bolt to the chest.

The Champions began to take down the droids in the similar fashion as before. Randy noticed the broken droids and sighed. His hands sparked with more lightning as he blasted the team across the area. Norland stood up and Randy fired another bolt toward him. Holding the lightning on Norland, electrocuting him. Norland fought back to his feet, pressing against the lightning blasting his chest. The weight of the lightning was heavy to Norland's strength. Norland reached closer to Randy and as he came closer, he raised up his fist, punching Randy and kicking him back.

"You want to keep this going?" Norland asked.

"Nah." Randy said. "Not right now."

Norland's hands turned blue. Randy stood still, gazing up to the air and quickly a large lightning bolt came down over Randy as Norland fired a lightning bolt of his own. After the bolt and crashed, Randy was gone as were the droids. Norland looked around, seeing no one as the Champions stood up.

"Where'd he go?" Norland asked.

'Back to Judge." Nader said. "He had to."

"Why run?" Sarge asked. "He could've remained here like a man."

"We have to think like Judge. This whole thing was a distraction. Seemly to weaken us. It's one of Judge's tricks."

"We should go to Centro." Norland said. "Confront Judge before he does this again."

"I think not. Going on his turf will only end in death. Our death."

"Then, what do you have planned? Because, we need eyes everywhere if this is to continue."

Nader nodded. Thinking.

"I'll make a call." Nader said, returning inside the base.

Nixon approached Norland, looking at Nader and Sarge returning to the headquarters. The rest of the Champions stood outside with Norland.

"What do we do?"

"We see who Nader calls. Maybe they can find a solution to this whole thing."

"And if they don't?"

"Then, we'll do things ourselves. As before."

Nixon nodded with a sincere look.

"Yes sir."

Everyone returned inside the base. Norland remained outside, looking at his hands returning to their natural color. He gazed at the ground, seeing the large scorched mark from the lightning bolt where Randy stood. He sighed.

IV

AN ENGLISH ASSISTANCE

Hours have passed since the attack at the headquarters. Inside, agents scatter gaining more details on Judge's whereabouts and his next phase of attack. The Champions stayed to themselves, however, Norland walked down a hallway, reaching Nader's office. Nader hung up the phone as Norland entered.

"How's finding the help?" Norland asked.

"He's on the way." Nader replied.

"He? Mind if I who he is?"

"He's just like you. An English version of you some would say. He should be here soon. You can question him after his arrival."

"Fair enough."

Walking toward the entrance, a white hoverjet appeared and landed. Coming out of the jet was a brown-haired man dressed in military gear similar to Norland and of the same age. The only exception was of the British flag on the left side of his chest. He approached both Norland and Nader. Shaking Nader's hand.

"You came quick." Nader said.

"I had to after what I heard. But, I'm here to help."

"Commander Norland meet Austin Ehrenreich or as his

codename states, Commander England.”

“Commander England?” Norland said.

“Don’t blame me. I didn’t approve of the name. did you approve of Norland?”

“No. It was just a calling as one would say.”

“Makes two of us.”

“Let’s head inside and give you all the details we know, Mr. Ehrenreich.”

They entered the headquarters. Everyone placed their gaze upon Ehrenreich. He waved toward them with a smile.

“Follow me.” Nader said.

He followed Norland and Nader into the office. Professor Flm walked by to see Ehrenreich sitting down at the table. Norland caught him and nodded. Flm nodded back and continued with his business.

“I have to ask.” Ehrenreich said. “Who is this Sinister Judge guy?”

“He’s a dictator from Centro.” Nader said. “A country not known to the world yet. However, with his attack on our base, he’s making himself known.”

“That’s intriguing. How come he waited until now?”

“Information we received from someone details this isn’t Judge’s first attack of the year. He attacked the Citadel of Enchantment a few months ago where Mr. Donald Fortune resides. Fortune wasn’t harmed in the events. But, Judge knew how to get him and when. The same goes to us.”

“Like he knows our every move.” Norland said. “We need to go to him, Nader.”

“Going into Centro would be the act of a terrorist and would play Canada at risk with the U.N. Something I highly choose to avoid.”

"So, how are we going to stop him from doing these attacks?"

"Track his movement. Steady."

"How when he knows our move?" Norland asked. "he sent someone here with an army of his droids. How soon will he do so again?"

"Play by the news, Commander."

"I'll play as long as he's stopped."

Norland stood up from his seat and left the office. Nader shook his head and Ehrenreich was confused.

"What's his issue?"

"He's not used to doing things by the book."

"I heard about what happened in Retropolis. How he was there to protect the city and the people. Maybe you should let him take his team over to Judge's turf. See what happens."

"Not taking that chance. Better if Judge comes onto our turf rather than us on his."

Three women enter the headquarters as Norland walked back into the lobby area. They approached him.

"You're Commander Norland."

"I am. And you're?"

"Agent Jessica Mara. We didn't get to meet due to the Retropolis incident. I was a witness to Noldar and Death stealing the artifacts."

"I'm sure they're in a safer place now."

"Mariah Cooper. I'm working alongside Jessica on this whole Judge thing."

"We're trying our best. As it seems."

Norland glanced at the third woman. Different from the agents. She wore a militaristic uniform with metallic gauntlets on her arms. He silver-like hair stood out from the others.

"I've never seen you before." Norland said.

"Sonya Rowlings."

"Enemies call her the Lady Siren."

"Lady Siren? How come?"

"My skill set isn't what they perceive it to be."

"Let's hope you use it."

"You'll see."

In Judgedath, Centro. Judge sat as another individual entered his throne room. Dressed in all white with a robe and pants with a hood covering his face. Randy stood in the throne room next to Judge.

"Abin-Qa." Judge said. "You received my word."

"I did. Figured things would be a little complicated. Myself meeting you on your grounds."

"I understand you caution. But, I have a proposition that will benefit us both."

"What kind of proposition do you have in mind?"

"Help me bring about a new Albion into the world. An empire that all nations will fear."

"Funny. Wouldn't that make me your enemy?"

"Depends on your next words for this offer."

"What do I need to do?"

"Aid myself and Thunderstorm in eliminating the ones thwarting the plan. Commander Norland, his Champions, and T.I.T.A.N."

"And what do I receive my I agree to this offer?"

"Richness even your country doesn't possess."

Abin paced slowly in the throne room. Randy's hands were steady with small streaks of lightning coming from his fingertips. Judge sat quietly, waiting for an answer from the Middle Eastern ruler. Abin nodded, turning toward Judge.

"I will gather my Desert Vipers and we will be waiting on the word."

Judge nodded with a glint.

"Excellent."

V

<u>JUDGMENTAL WARFARE</u>

Sinister Judge's forces returned to the headquarters, startling them once more. Nader, Ehrenreich, Lady Siren, Norland, and his Champions all headed outside to confront the visitors. This time, the judgedroids were not with Thunderstorm. Abin-Qa stood with them.

"I've heard about your base being attacked continually. I just had to come and see for myself."

"Who are you?" Norland asked. "Where's Randy Keith and Judge?"

"I will answer in reverse. Randy and Judge are not here. They remain in Centro. However, working with Judge has given me the opportunity to do something greater for my people."

"And your people are?" Nader asked.

"Those in the Asia Minor. Struggling every day because of foreign countries and paid-off betrayers. I am Altair Masculine. Known in my region as Abin-Qa. Today, I begin to make my mark on the world. By taking T.I.T.A.N. down with Canada's most noble Commander."

"I don't see how that will work." Norland said. "We've had our share against the droids."

"I wasn't referring to the droids."

Rising up from the shadows across the entire base were soldiers carrying blades and dressed in garments blending them in with the ground. They appeared as living sand. They surrounded the team quickly. Weapons up and ready.

"I was speaking of my Desert Vipers. They've helped me along the way to make my region safer for those who cannot defend themselves."

"Must be nice." Nixon uttered.

"It is. For us."

Norland's hands glowed blue and the icy cool air released from them. Ice formed over his hands. Abin-Qa noticed and pointed. The Vipers also were uneasy.

"What's with his hands?" Ehrenreich noticed. Pointing at Norland.

"Commander." Nader said. "What's going on?"

"We need to take them out." Norland said. "On my signal."

Norland blasted the droids with a ice-lightning bolt.

"Whoa." Siren said.

The Champions rushed toward the Vipers. Fighting them across the grounds. Nader fired shots toward Abin-Qa, however he managed to dodge the bullets and threw a dagger, hitting Nader in the arm. Siren rushed toward Qa with twirls of kicks. He wasn't even hit and shoved Siren to the ground. Ehrenreich hovered into the air and dove down, punching the ground where Abin-Qa stood, causing a tremor. Qa fell to the ground as Norland and Ehrenreich surrounded him. He scoffed.

"You're done." Ehrenreich said.

"Not quite." Abin-Qa replied, tossing a grenade into the air.

"Everybody down!" Norland yelled.

Norland grabbed the grenade and held it to his chest. After three seconds, the grenade exploded, knocking Norland back into the headquarters through the glass. The grenade blasted an electrical energy. The Champions rushed in to assist their leader as QA and his Vipers vanished into the ground. Norland arose.

"I've had enough of this."

"We all have." Nixon said.

"We need to play this by the books." Nader said. "It's our only way of getting to Judge."

"No. no we don't." Norland replied. "The books are going to be tossed out for this."

"Don't do anything foolish, Commander."

"I already have."

Norland shook himself from the electricity and stood up. Walking away. Nixon nodded to the team and followed Norland into a ifferent room of the headquarters.

Norland sat against the table as Nixon approached him.

"I know you're thinking of a plan. Tell me what it is."

"You already know the answer." Norland said.

"When do we head out?"

"As soon as it quiets down out there. You know where the nearest hoverjet is?"

"I do."

"Good. Tell the others. Let them know."

"Yes sir."

Nixon left the room as Norland sat down in the nearby chair and sighed. Looking at his hands. He could feel the icy temperature flowing through them.

VI

<u>DIVINE OVER TECH</u>

Once things quieted down at the headquarters, Norland and the Champions made their exit as the hoverjet awaited them. As they proceeded to enter, Nader, Ehrenreich, and Siren came out of the building toward them.

"The hell is this?!" Nader yelled.

"Our way of doing things." Norland said. "It's the only way, Nader."

"Where are you going?" Siren asked.

"To Centro. Visit Judge on his own turf. He's sent his attacks our way enough times already and he's done it in quick procession. I can't allow another attack to occur. Me and my team are going into Judgedath to confront Judge and end this whole Albion plan of his."

Nader stared. Siren and Ehrenreich nodded.

"Then I'm coming along." Siren said.

Nader turned to her. She glanced at him and focused on Norland.

"You're sure about this?"

"I've seen what you can do. I'm in."

"Then, count me in as well." Ehrenreich added. "You'll need some extra strength in getting into a place like Centro."

Norland nodded with a smile and looked at Nader. Nader didn't smile, but gave him a quick nod.

"Don't bring trouble our way with this."

"We won't" Norland replied.

Siren and Ehrenreich entered the hoverjet. Nader stepped back as the jet lifted up from the ground and took off. Watching it leave, Nader returned inside the headquarters.

In the air, Norland gathered his team around with Siren and Ehrenreich present.

"When we arrive in Centro, remember, we're in the enemy territory. No civilian casualties. Only droids, Abin-Qa, his soldiers, and Thunderstorm. Sinister Judge is our target. We apprehend him by any means."

"Like kill him?" Nixon asked. "If it comes to that?"

"We do what we have to for the completion of this mission. It's all on us. Not T.I.T.A.N. Not the Canadian government nor any other government. This is our task and our task alone."

Ehrenreich nodded.

"I understand."

Norland nodded.

"Thank you for that."

Norland walked away and sat to himself. Entering a state of meditation. Through his mediation process, he found himself back in a place where snow fell continually. Walking around the snowy grounds, he gazed upon the presence of Lord Blizzard.

"You are entering a dire place, Adam Watson."

"I have no other choice. Sinister Judge must be

apprehended."

"But, you have not met Judge face to face. Nor experienced his full power. He is not like Black Sector. Nor is he like Noldar or Death. He is someone far stronger and smarter."

"Then, what must I do?"

"Use the power I've given you. Use it wisely. For Judge has power of his own. One he acquired from a very dark source. Your team and new allies will prove useful in this coming fight. Just keep your mind clear and focused."

"Will do."

Norland arose out of his meditation to find Siren at his side.

"You do that often?" She asked.

"What?"

"Meditate."

"When I can."

"Does it work for you?"

"It has its purposes."

"And are your abilities part of the purpose?"

"In a way they are."

"Good to know."

"Why did you want to come with us?"

"Because this is a mission that must be completed. I'm a mission girl. I go to where an unfinished mission is available, and I assist until it's done."

"And you want to help us stop Judge?"

"Of course. It's part of the mission."

Norland smiled. Siren smiled back as she walked away.

VII

<u>JUDGMENT TO COME</u>

The hoverjet made its arrival in Centro. The sky covered in clouds of darkness. The team looked out as the flew over a cornfield. Seeing farmers reaping the corn. The farmers gazed up and waved.

"We know he's not the only one living here." Norland said. "They're civilians here."

"The plan still stays?" Nixon asked.

"Yeah."

Flying over, they reach the city of Judgedath and in the horizon stood a large palace. Medieval appearance struck out the most amongst every other building in the city.

"I take it that's where he resides." Woody said.

"This place looks spooky." Andrea said. "Look at the fog around the place."

"Find a landing spot." Norland commanded. "Once we're on foot, we'll discuss plans of an ambush. I prefer we do this as stealthy as possible. He cannot know how many of us have come."

"What if he already knows we're here?" Ehrenreich asked. "I mean all of us. There's no way we came flying into his air zone without him knowing."

"We'll find out once we see him."

Securing a small place near the palace, the hoverjet landed. The team stepped out onto the stone grounds. Staring at the palace, which stood tall in front of them. Gazing up at its height.

"Who built this place?" Siren wondered.

"Those who came before." Norland said. "Always them."

"Now what's the plan?" Ehrenreich asked.

"Me and the Champions will enter the palace to confront Judge. You and Siren keep watch. Thunderstorm and Abin-Qa are sure to be here. Also, keep a look out for Judge's droids and Qa's sand-soldiers."

"Copy that." Siren said.

Norland nodded. He and the Champions made their way toward the palace doors while Ehrenreich and Siren stood next to the jet. Opening the large double-doors, creaking as they entered the palace and the first thing to capture their glance was Judge himself, sitting on the throne.

"You've come." Judge said. "All of you."

The doors shut behind them. The Champions turned back as the doors closed while Norland's eyes were locked on Judge.

"So, this is how you appear in person."

"What did you expect? I have my ways of perception."

"Why attack the base? Why continuously?"

"Because it was the only way to get your attention. I knew if I were to show up at the headquarters, I would be breaking government law. However, the point was simple. I need T.I.T.A.N. and you out of the way to fully execute my plan."

"Building a new Albion?"

"Yes."

"Funny. You attack me, my team, and T.I.T.A.N. only. But, what about the others out there. Roaming around cities and countries. How come you haven't confronted them as you did us?"

"I had a recent encounter with one of those scattered ones. We share a familiar ground when it comes to sorcery."

"I was told you attack a man at his home. You did the same to us."

"True. But, the attacks were far different from one another. I sent my droids out the base to attack you. While I sent a much darker force to harm the other. It is a way of doing matters justly."

"And you seek to judge us as you did him?"

"His judgment isn't complete. Neither are yours."

From the surrounding walls came down judgedroids. Circling the team. Norland looked over to Nixon. Giving him a nod. Nixon began shooting at the droids with his shotgun. Andrea pulled out her whips, striking the droids. The Champions combated against the oncoming army of judgedroids from the walls. Norland and Judge kept their eyes on one another. Meanwhile, outside Ehrenreich and Siren can hear the commotion of the fight.

"We need to get in there." Siren said.

Walking to the palace doors, they were stopped by the sound of thunder in the sky. Turning around to find Thunderstorm and Abin-Qa standing before them.

"Better if we're out here." Ehrenreich said, looking at the two associates of Judge.

The fighting continued inside the palace. Judge arose from his throne, stepping forward facing Norland. Norland stood still as his hands began to glow.

"I've read up on you, Commander Norland. Learned of your encounter with a divine force. How you said he granted you such power. What has it become ever since?"

"You want to find out, eh?"

"I believe I can achieve more with such power if I can take it from you."

"Give it your best shot!"

Norland rushed toward Judge, striking him in the chest and face with punches laced with the icy power. Judge did not move from the strikes and backslapped Norland against the wall.

"I have little respect for those who do not know their place."

Judge charged up his hands and fired a blast of energy onto Norland. Piercing him on his back. He yelled as he tried standing up. Andrea turned around, seeing Norland fighting Judge. She ran over, whipping one of Judge's hands from Norland and he stood up, kicking Judge. Pulling the whip back, Judge grabbed it without haste and injected his own energy into the whip, electrocuting Andrea.

She fell to the round as Norland grabbed Judge, shoving him against the wall and pummeling him. The droids were all defeated as the palace doors burst open with Ehrenreich rolling in, followed by a hovering electrocuting Thunderstorm. Siren faced Abin-Qa outside.

"Fitting how I can take out more than one hero." Thunderstorm uttered. "This is my kind of day."

Siren turned and fired a needle into the back of Thunderstorm's neck. Feeling the sting, he fell to the floor, pulling the needle from his neck and staring at Siren.

"Bitch. What did you do to me?"

"Something to slow you down for a moment."

Thunderstorm went to release a lightning blast on Siren, but his power wasn't working. Unsure, he glanced at the needle and back to Siren, who smiled. From behind, Ehrenreich arose and lunged Thunderstorm into the air and crashing him down. Abin-Qa noticed Norland facing Judge and vanished from the area. Judge laughed, finding himself surrounded by everyone.

"As it shall be. Everyone will submit to Judge in due time."

"I don't think so."

"Oh, it doesn't matter. For I have seen the future and what is to come. A dark future. One of betrayal within your own countrymen. Friends will fight against friends. Brothers and sisters will be at war. Cosmic forces shall return. Human technology will evolve and become greater than they could imagine. One where heroes will kill each other for justice and vengeance. A future where the true darkness of the universe shall rise again and have dominion over all the earth."

"Why are you telling us this?" Norland wondered.

"For I have seen that future and it cannot be altered. Nor can anything before it be changed. it is written. Written in the tables of creation. The end is coming sooner than you can imagine."

"It won't stop us from winning this fight." Siren said.

"Believe me, you will win some and lose some. Just as I. but, in the end, we all will see who's on one side or the other. It is all that truly matters. For it is just."

"You're coming with us." Norland said.

He grabbed Judge by his cloak and without recognizing, Judge warped into transparent matter and vanished from their sight with a flash of white light. They looked around the throne room and Judge was gone.

"Where'd he go?" Ehrenreich asked.

"What kind of man are we dealing with?" Nixon wondered. "What was all that about the future?"

"I don't know."

Helping a weakened Andrea up to her feet, they returned to the hoverjet and left the city of Judgedath and the country of Centro.

Returning to T.I.T.A.N. headquarters, Andrea is taken to the doctor. Norland told Nader all about their encounter with Judge. How he knew of their arrival to his strange disappearance. Nader nodded as Norland told him everything he knew.

"He'll pop up again." Nader said.

"And when he does?"

"We'll be prepared for that day. But, concerning this future he spoke of, I don't know what to tell you."

"He seemed pretty clear about it. I can tell in his voice, he wasn't lying nor was he creating a story for us to hear. If he can do what I saw, I can believe he's witnessed the future. Just don't know how."

"Don't concern yourself over it. The present is now. The future is tomorrow. Focus on one day at a time."

"Understand." Norland said with a smile.

Nader left the office, leaving Norland alone. There, Norland mediated on Judge's words and took out his phone to dial a number. The number of which he dialed belonged to Kenari Clark.

THE UNSTOPPABLE BEAST: INCARNATION

I

OBSESSION OF ONE'S DESIRE

General Lawler entered a military base in the outskirts of New York City. Inside, he walked by soldiers and lieutenants discussing matters. He walked into another room. A laboratory as he approached the scientist who stood next to eh table.

"Ahem." Lawler said.

"Oh. I'm sorry. I didn't even notice you come in."

"Are you him?"

"Am I who?"

"Dr. Edward Bohr. The scientist from New York?"

"That would be me."

"You look a little younger than I expected. Thought you would be much older. Experienced."

"Don't judge the age of the scientist, my friend."

"I'm not your friend."

"Noted." Bohr replied quietly.

"Then, you know why I'm here today."

"I have an idea."

"I hear you're a fan of the Beast."

"You mean The Unstoppable Beast. Yes, I am a fan." Lawler looked down and shook his head.

"Pity."

"Why?"

"Because you're here not to be a fan. But a scientist and we have something you might be interested in."

A soldier entered the lab, handing Lawler a briefcase. The soldier left as Lawler opened the case, showing Bohr what laid inside. He saw a capsule and there was blood within it. Bohr pointed as his finger started to shake.

"Is that what I think it is?"

"It is. Blood from the Beast himself."

"Greatness."

"We need you for a secret project that depends on this blood."

"What do I receive if I agree to help?"

"More than you know. Hell, you might meet the Beast if you agree."

"Seriously?"

"Only time will tell. You have until tomorrow morning to give us an answer. Take the time to think on it. Your future and your life depend on it."

Lawler left the laboratory as Bohr contained himself glaring at the blood capsule. Following the next day, Lawler retuned to the lab and found Bohr already at work with the blood. He grinned.

"I see you're taking a like to it."

"I am. Truly."

"So, you will help us?"

"Yes, General. I will."

"Good. We'll be giving you a bodyguard for your work. We believe you'll need it if Kent Brock finds out you have his blood."

"I'm sorry." Bohr said. "Who is Kent Brock?"

"Why you're his biggest fan. He's the Beast."

"I don't understand the terminology of that statement." Bohr mentioned. "How is he the Beast?"

"Study his blood. You may learn that before we do."

"But how?"

"It lives within him. That's all we've come to know. Study his blood and you might learn much more and what it's capable of."

"Yes sir. Will do."

Lawler nodded, leaving the lab. Bohr returned to his work. Confused and curious as he stared at the blood of the Beast.

II

LEADING THOSE ASTRAY

Bohr continued his study of the blood. However, he was unaware of Charlotte Lawler's involvement with the blood. She was responsible for having it as General Lawler discovered, taking the blood sample from Charlotte and giving it to Bohr. Now, Charlotte has traveled to tell Kent Brock of the news concerning his blood.

Sitting with James Porter in his home, Charlotte told Kent of the news. Taking it highly serious, Kent paced around the living room.

"We can get it back, Kent." charlotte said. "Just trust me."

"How did he even know you had a sample of my blood?"

"I don't know. I never told him of it."

"He must have found out from someone on the outside." James said. "It had to be some soldier who saw us."

"When did you take the sample?" Kent asked.

"When we were in Dallas. Sometime after the whole fight between the Beast and Sean Hancock."

"A soldier there must've seen you with the sample and gave Lawler the word on it."

"Perhaps."

"There is no other way I can see this." James said. "Now, we need to find a way to get back his blood before some scientist takes it and starts experiments."

"It's what they want." Kent said. "They want to start experiments. Humans, animals, it doesn't matter. They want to replicate he Beast and create an army with it."

"Sound cliché man." James scoffed.

"I know it does, but it's the true. Nothing is new."

"I can take the trip to the base. Speak to him about where the blood has been taken."

"No. I have a better idea."

"Oh, this I would like to hear." James laughed.

"You're not going to like it."

They left Porter's home and traveled to the base.

Upon making their arrival, the three walked onto the military grounds. Quickly being surrounded by armed men, General Lawler walked outside of the base, seeing the three. He sighed as he made his way toward them.

"This is a bold move." Lawler said, walking towards them. "Very bold."

"I had to take a chance." Kent said.

"Why are you three here?"

"I know you have a sample of my blood. I demand to have it back."

"I'm sorry, Mr. Brock. But, that sample is now property of the U.S. Government. You cannot have it back, I'm afraid."

"It wasn't yours to take. You have no idea what you're messing with."

"I know exactly what I'm up to. Your blood will be the key to solving a puzzle I've dreamed of since I began the field."

"You're making a terrible mistake." Charlotte said.

"Young one, take your boyfriend and his friend on home. Before we have to move to desperate measures."

"He threatened us?" James said. "How dare you sir."

"How dare you for trespassing onto government property."

Kent looked around, looking for an opening into the base. He appeared to spot one near the left side of the base, a place where cargo is dropped off. He nodded.

"Alright. We'll go."

"But, what about your blood?" Charlotte asked.

"Don't worry about it. Sorry for this little disturbance."

Kent turned Charlotte and James around, walking away from the base. As they were no longer seen, Kent pointed toward the cargo section. Signaling a way of entry. They agreed and snuck into the base. Reaching further inside, Kent looked around and found the laboratory. Bolting inside, he confronted Bohr and saw the blood capsule sitting at the table.

"Who are you?" Bohr asked.

"I'm the man who's blood you're working on."

"You're… You're the Beast!" Bohr yelled. "I mean he's within you right now!"

"What?" Kent said with confusion.

"I'm a big fan. A very big fan of the Beast. Tell me, how does it work?"

"How does what work?"

"The transformation. Is it painful or is it steady?"

"It's painful. I wouldn't wish it on anyone."

"Oh. But, I'm sure the power you feel is impressive."

"Enough talk. Just hand me the capsule and I'll be out of here."

"I will do no such thing."

"Or what?"

"You'll have to deal with my bodyguard."

Bohr pointed and Kent turned around to see his bodyguard. A tall man, looking down at Kent. He was built and chiseled.

"Intriguing." Kent said. "There's something off about you."

"Care to find out." The bodyguard said, touching the wall.

"What in the hell?"

The bodyguard's body had morphed into the same texture as the wall. Color and all. Kent couldn't believe it. Nor could Bohr.

"Friends call me the Absorption."

"I can see why."

Absorption backhanded Kent against the laboratory wall. Charlotte ran toward him, checking him. Absorption and Bohr stood and watched as Lawler ran into the lab, seeing Kent on the ground.

"The hell happened?!" Lawler asked.

"He was threatening the scientist." Absorption said. "I had to knock him back."

"Oh god." Lawler uttered. "Do you know what you've done?"

"What?"

Kent rose up, shaking, Charlotte could only stare at him.

Kent, what's wrong?"

"The pain. It's consuming me. He's coming out."

"No. No." Charlotte said. "Fight him. Fight him, Kent."

"I can't. He's too strong."

Kent's arms started shaking as dark gray hair began to grow upon them. Lawler ran over and grabbed Charlotte, leaving the lab. Absorption and Bohr stood watching Kent transform in pain as the Beast overcame him. His height increasing, the hair growing. Soldiers surrounded the lab as the Beast was fully manifested, turning around to roar at the adversaries. Staring at them with his dark red eyes.

"He really is the Beast." Bohr uttered.

"The hell!" Absorption yelled.

The Beast lunged toward Absorption, slamming him through the wall. Soldiers surrounded the two as they fought. Absorption using the concrete floors to combat the Beast. Meanwhile, Bohr took a sample of the blood, after it was tested with some other chemicals suited for medical treatment. Taking the sample, he injected it into himself. The blood of the Beast circulated through him. Within seconds, Bohr fell to the ground in immense sharp pain.

The Beast ransacked the soldiers around him before pummeling Absorption into the concrete floors. After the fight, the Beast bolted to the outside, escaping the military facility. The soldiers make their moves to chase him and Bohr remained inside the lab, laying on the floor twitching.

III

THE MASTER, THE LEADER, THE RULER

While the military tracked down the Beast into the wilderness, Bohr remained in the lab. As the sharp pains receded, Bohr arose from the floor a changed indicial. Due to the injection of the blood, Bohr's intellect had increased. He could feel the change within him and as he went to place his hand on the table, he pushed the table into the floor.

"Wow."

Knowing he has similar feats of the Beast, including his strength. Bohr left the laboratory. Soldiers stood I front of him.

"Where are you going?"

"To get some air."

"Orders are to keep you in the lab until the General is done with you."

"I am done with him. Now move out of my way."

Bohr raised his hands, swiping the soldiers from his presence without a touch. He stopped and stared at his hand. Nodding.

"Impressive. With this gift I have been given, I can be a master among the people. A leader to them. A true ruler."

Standing outside the base, Bohr realized he was no longer the same. He walked away from the base a new creature.

IV

FREE WILL

The Beast managed to escape the soldiers and found himself near a shack deep in the wilderness. Stopping, he sat down and immediately transformed back into Kent. There, Kent sat in the shack until it was the following day. Once he awoke from his deep sleep, he made his travels to a small town nearby where he was picked up by James.

Charlotte learned of Kent's whereabouts sometime after as did General Lawler. Though, many was investigating the current whereabouts of Bohr, who was no longer seen by anyone near the base ever since he left.

While Kent remained at James' place, he wondered to himself concerning his bond with the Beast. He nodded as James approached him.

"You're in some deep thinking, aren't you?"

"In a matter. I've learned one thing about this whole thing between me and the Beast within. Free will determines our fate. Both mine and his."

In a distant place far from the military facility, Bohr stood on a hill, overlooking a large metropolitan city in the distance. Its skyscrapers increased his interest of the place.

"This city will be the first phase of my ruler ship. I will rule over this place and it shall spread. Spread like a benevolent virus across the world. I will be its Ruler. No matter the outcome. For I am the outcome."

THE RESISTANCE: THE STROH DYNASTY

I

DISTURBANCE

Weeks after their own solo journeys, a call was made to Colonel Evan Nader of a hidden weapons trade taking place between militia groups and criminal elements intergraded into various countries. Nader considered to release T.I.TA.N. agents into the field, once he learned of technology similar to the attack on Retropolis months back. Nader made call to Kenari Clark and Nathan Hawke. They rallied up themselves and their allies. The Resistance formed again.

Traveling to a distant facility in the wilderness of Canada, The Resistance moved with haste and stealth. The Swordman, Commander Norland took the ground as Taltus The Powerman, Nano Man, and Theus took the sky. Moving through the area, soldiers came forth from the facility, firing energy weapons toward the team. The Swordman, riding the Land-Dagger, looked out toward the militia soldiers.

"Norland, take them out."

"Will do."

Norland sped over on his motorcycle, conjuring a bolt

of icy lightning from the sky, freezing the soldiers in place.

"Watch it now, we're right above you." Nano Man uttered.

"Where's the Beast?" Theus asked. "I haven't seen him out here."

"Oh, he's here. Just you wait."

More soldiers burst from the facility doors and immediately, The Unstoppable Beast appeared. Roaring as the soldiers ran from his presence. He smacked them across the woods and chased others into the forest. Meanwhile, Theus and Taltus hovered over the facility.

"Strike it." Nano Man said.

Theus shot down a large thunderbolt while Taltus used his lightning vision to open a hole into the facility. As the beams melted the roof, it caved in, falling on those who were still inside. Taltus flew into the facility with Theus and Nano Man following. On the ground, Swordman and Norland reached the front gate, blowing it down with a blast from Swordman's land-dagger. Entering the facility grounds, hey kicked in the door.

"Which way is the location?" Norland asked.

"This way."

They walked down the corridor and came across the area where Taltus and Theus busted in. Nano Man landed as they entered the room. A room covered with technology of weaponized energy. Nano Man's helmet opened by the receding of the sides, revealing Nathan's face as he took a closer look at the tech. The Swordman approached him.

"You recognize any of this?"

"I do. Same tech from those guys we fought months back. I don't know how they got their hands on it."

"What about Kex Kendrick?" Norland asked. "His

associates?”

“Not possible.” Taltus said. “His associates left Enigma City after Kex was taken to prison. They can’t be involved in this.”

“Then who?” Nathan wondered. “What shall we do about this, Ken?”

“Split it up between myself and you. We’ll have to keep this contained ourselves.”

“I thought T.I.T.A.N. was coming to take what was left.” Norland said. “What will I tell them?”

“Tell them the truth.” The Swordman said. “We took it for a safer keep.”

Norland nodded.

“By the way.” Nathan said. “I’m having a party tonight and you’re all invited.”

“A party?” Theus said. “Sounds particularly intriguing.”

“You know I don’t do parties, Nate.” The Swordman said.

“Just this once.”

“No. I have matters to attend to back in Retropolis.”

“I thought you handed the whole turf war between the crime lords.”

“I did. But, there are other matters occurring and I can’t keep them going pass.”

Nathan nodded with a smirk.

“I get it. Well, I’ll tell the others you were busy handling some Retropolis work.”

“Best decision.”

The Swordman and Nathan gathered all the tech.

“We need to move out.” Swordman said.

“As he said.” Nathan said.

The Resistance walked out of the base as The Beast

returned. He stopped in front of the team.

"He seems calmer than our previous encounter." Theus said.

"He's more so of the same." Nathan said. "However, he's learning his place."

The Beast approached Nathan.

"Hey, you're free to go. All the guys have been taken care of."

The Beast nodded toward the team and left. The Swordman sat onto his motorcycle as did Norland with his. Nathan's mask closed up, hovering into the air with Taltus and Theus.

"We did good today." The Swordman said.

"We did." Norland replied.

"Don't get soft on us now." Nathan laughed.

The Resistance left the base. Empty and silent.

Later that night, Nathan held a party at his residence, and many were in attendance. Including Norland, Taltus, and Theus. Kent Brock did not attend and neither did The Swordman. Alice Jacobs approached Nathan, looking out at the large crowd of visitors.

"You have this under control?" She asked.

"As best as I can." Nathan laughed.

"Where's the other guy?"

"Handling some matters back at his place. Don't worry, he knew about this."

"I see."

Meanwhile, in Retropolis, The Swordman chased down

some criminals with relations to Sir Onyx and J. strangely enough, the criminals were working on both sides of the turf war.

"Why are you still here?" Swordman asked.

"Just some last-minute deals had to be made!"

"The deals are canceled. Leave this place before you meet the Creator."

The criminals took off without hesitation and didn't bother to look back. The Swordman returned to the Rapid-Blade when he felt a strange energy source in the air. He gazed around and noticed a peculiar event taking place in the sky, far above the clouds. He watched as the colors moved like explosions. Silent explosions. The air went chilly and small drops of rain started to fall.

"Hmm." The Swordman uttered.

<u>SEARCHING THE SKIES</u>

The following day, Kenari visited Nathan at his mansion. Entering the place, Alice walked by and approached him.

"Mr. Clark. I wasn't expecting to see you here."

"I came to speak with Nate. Something's come up."

"He's in the bunker."

"Thank you."

"By the way, I didn't see you at the party last night."

"I had some business to deal with back in Retropolis."

"Hope it worked out."

Kenari nodded, walking down the hallway toward the nano-bunker. The doors opened and Kenari saw Nathan working on some nanotech equipment. Kenari knocked, getting Nathan's attention. Causing Nathan to jump and turn.

"Seriously."

"Had to let you know I was in."

"Oh. Could've called ahead of time." Nathan remarked. "So, why are you here? Strange to see you."

"While you were having your party, I saw something in the sky last night."

"Saw what?"

"There's something taking place in the atmosphere. I was interrogating some of Onyx and J's men to where I noticed something occurring in the heavens."

"The heavens? So, Jesus is coming back, huh?"

"He's coming. But, not at the moment."

"What's your plan on figuring it out?"

"Where's Taltus and Theus?"

"Taltus returned to his fortress while Theus is scouting the earth. Looking for any other militia bases we may have missed."

Kenari nodded.

"Good to hear. Contact them and let them know. Better they search the sky rather than the two of us."

"Why is that?"

"We're human. They're not."

Nathan took note and smirked. Kenari left the bunker while Nathan went back to his work.

Later in the hours, Taltus and Theus received word from Nathan to search the sky. In doing so, Kenari prepared himself in his Swordman gear and headed out, looking up to see Taltus and Theus flying by. Nathan put on his Nano Man armor and followed them. In the sky, above the clouds, Taltus and Theus felt a strange disturbance moving through the air.

"It's strong." Theus said. "But, familiar in a way. Similar to those in my realm."

"You too?" Taltus said. "Reminds me of Olympus. But, stranger."

Through the clouds came a burst of cold air, knocking Taltus and Theus from their balance. Nano Man could feel it passing him. The Swordman also felt the chill.

"Nathan, what is it?"

"It's something not from here. The air is strange."

As the air passed, a large metallic object appeared before Taltus and Theus. Slowly descending to the earth.

"By Eden!" Theus said. "What is that?"

"I do not know." Taltus replied.

Swordman gazed up to the sky once more, now seeing the metallic object. Nano Man also saw it and flew closer.

"Nathan, be careful." The Swordman said.

"Don't worry. I'll be fine."

Nano Man bolted toward the object with Taltus and Theus to follow. Getting closer, Nano Man learned it was not a simple object. The markings on the side revealed much more to him than what could be seen from the ground.

"Guys, this is no ordinary object."

"What is it?" Swordman asked.

"It's a craft. Some kind of craft."

The large craft moved toward the ocean. Nano Man, Taltus, and Theus followed behind the object as Swordman followed from the ground. They watched as the craft landed on an island in the middle of the ocean. The surrounding areas were quickly hit with a shockwave. Silence covered the area as a door on the craft opened up, a figure walked out.

"I have come."

They watched as the tall figure exited the craft and looked out toward Newark. The figure wore sleek armor. Its colors were of emerald mixed with copper as were his eyes.

"We might have trouble." Nano Man uttered.

III

<u>WORKS OF THE CONQUEROR</u>

The figure from the craft continued to step forward, now walking upon the water of the sea.

"Ken, you're seeing this?" Nathan asked.

"Closely."

"This world is unlike what I've been told." The figure said with a chilling voice. "Now, I shall do what I came to do."

"We need to confront him." Taltus said.

"Are you sure about that?" Nathan asked.

"Give it a try." The Swordman said. "See how he'll react. He hasn't seen us yet."

"Ugh. Sure thing."

Nano Man, Taltus, and Theus made their move toward the figure. Approaching him as he stood motionless on the water. They circled him. His eyes were instantly placed on the three heroes while The Swordman came across on a metallic boat moving across the water.

"What is he?" Swordman asked.

"He's organic." Nano Man said. "I'm sensing some technological effects to his body. His suit is filled with it. Tech not from our world."

"I have an audience."

"In a way." Nano Man uttered. "We saw you come from the sky."

"It was the only way into your world. Portals can be strange at times."

"You came through a portal?" Theus asked. "What portal?"

"One I conjured myself."

"Where are you from?" Taltus asked. "Olympus?"

"No. I do not come from the lineage of Zeus. I come from a realm hidden from humanity since the time of the Deluge."

"Ok, you're going pretty far into history now."

"The question was asked. I am only providing the answer."

"Noted. Your name?"

"Stroh. King Stroh. The Conqueror."

"Conqueror?" Nano Man said. "What have you conquered?"

"Many worlds. That is why I've come. To conquer this one."

"We have a problem with that." Taltus said.

"As will many. It is the purpose of my creation."

Pods opened upon the craft and spawns of robotic entities rush out into the air, scattered across the sky. Stroh gazed up toward them as did the others.

"What is he planning?" Swordman questioned.

"Go into the world, my children. Prepare them for your master's rule!"

The entities took off from the city in many directions.

"Taltus, Theus, follow one of the patterns!" The Swordman said. "Me and Nathan will handle Stroh."

"Will do." Taltus said.

Taltus and Theus took off after the trails. Moving like a bolt of lightning. Meanwhile, Swordman and Nano Man confronted Stroh as he stepped foot onto the pavement.

"You do not belong here." Swordman said.

"Oh, I do." Stroh replied. "It is my time to rule."

"I think not."

Nano Man blasted Stroh with an energy beam. However, Stroh kept his ground by absorbing the blast and retaliating it back to Nano Man. He flew across the pavement as Swordman lunged toward the Conqueror with his sword in hand. Swiping Stroh's arm, cutting him. Stroh was impressed but unharmed.

"Fitting. Such a weapon in the hands of your kind. Is…. Fascinating."

Stroh kicked Swordman back from his presence and evaporated into a digitized state. He was gone. Swordman rose up as Nano Man hovered toward him, looking around the area for Stroh.

"He's gone." Swordman said.

"What's next?"

"We need to contact Norland and Kent."

"I think we might need a little more assistance than the two of them."

Swordman nodded, placing his sword back onto the sheath.

"I'll make the call. See who answers like the last time."

"But, we need them here now. Not later."

"They'll get the message."

IV

<u>INTELLECT OVER STRENGTH</u>

Theus traveled oversees chasing down Stroh's droids while Taltus went north. Swordman contacted two helpers from across the States. Nano Man continued to find a way into Stroh's ship system. Few of the droids reached Toronto as commander Norland made himself known, taking down the droids with lightning blasts.

"Those are what he was speaking of." Norland said.

While gazing in the sky, Taltus appeared over him, coming down to the ground.

"Taltus."

"Commander Norland. I see you've met the droids."

"How many are there?"

"Hard to tell. Theus followed some over into the other countries."

"What about Swordman and Hawke?"

"They're trying to find a way into Stroh's ship."

"Stroh. He's the guy behind this?"

"He is. He's not from this world. He's from another dimension. Another place."

"Aren't they all these days."

Back in Newark, Silver Eagle and Bionic Rage have appeared to assist Swordman and Nano Man against the droids. Meanwhile, Stroh remained inside his ship, monitoring every location his droids traveled. He saw the occurrence in Toronto and smirked.

"Intriguing. A human working with a titagod."

Nano Man flew over toward Swordman as Silver Eagle fired machine gun rounds toward the droids nearby.

"We need Kent's Beast."

"I already give him word."

"And where is he?"

"Said he was near Toronto. He had a science meeting to attend there anyway. He should be helping Norland with the case."

"What about us? Rick and Rage are dealing with the droids."

"We find a way into his ship. Pull him out and end this nonsense."

"Agreed."

Norland and Taltus continued to take down the droids and from the streets emerged the Beast, roaring and crushing the droids.

"He came." Taltus said.

"I figured so." Norland replied. "We need him."

The Beast roared as he turned toward Taltus and Norland. They nodded. Stroh in his ship sees it and pressed a button. One droid laying down near the three heroes, gazed up and scanned both Taltus and the Beast. Norland ran over, stomping the droid's head.

"Guys, you're alright?"

Taltus and the Beast shook themselves around. Their eyes glowing the same color as the droids. Stroh laughed.

Both looked toward one another and clashed. Fighting each other against their own will.

"Dammit!" Norland said.

More droids came and Norland fought them off as Taltus and the Beast beat down one another under Stroh's control.

V

A WORLD CONQUERED

Due to the scattering of The Resistance, the droids have managed their own grid over the world, Stroh signaled the formation and caused an earthquake, moving across all the world.

"He's doing this." Swordman said.

He and Nano Man moved toward his ship. Eagle and Rage continue taking down the droids. Theus is over in London battling a few who are guarding the grid. Norland continued his fight in Toronto, while Taltus and the Beast continued their own scuffle.

Combining their own weapons, Swordman and Nano Man managed to break a hole into Stroh's ship and enter. Upon entering, they see its macabre interior design, glowing with a mix of organic and technology.

"I am impressed." Nano Man said.

"You would be."

Stroh appeared before them, warping fro the wall.

"You've entered. As I hoped."

"This has to end." Swordman declared. "No need to keep this going."

"I just started. Why should it end?"

"Because we have other things to end to." Nano Man

said.

"Be it so."

Stroh clashed with the two heroes. Forming two swords of his own, crawling out of his sleeves. He and Swordman clashed while Nano Man hovered above him with an energy blast. Stroh ricocheted the blast into Swordman. He fell as Stroh snatched Nano Man from the air, slamming him.

"The two of you cannot compare to what I know. The knowledge I possess. The strength I wield."

"Maybe so." The Swordman said. "But, we will not stop."

"I can see."

Swordman fired a dagger from his forearm into Stroh's control grid. Three seconds pass, and the grid exploded. Stroh turned quickly, running to the grid, trying to piece it back together. Meanwhile, his grid of droids fall to the earth. Taltus and the Beast cease their brawl and all the other droids collapse. A system error has hit Stroh's ship.

"No. what have you done?!"

"Put a stop to all of this. Wasting our time."

VI

THE COMING WARS

Stroh continued his panicking as Swordman approached him. Nano Man stood guard, his gauntlets energized and set to fire.

"This is over."

"For this day. But, I give you this warning."

"Another one of these." Nano Man said. "Convenient."

"My warnings are true. For I have seen them. Warnings from your near and distant futures. The first shall be of technology turning against you, the second will cause a conflict between your fellow allies, surging into a war unlike any you have entered, the last, the last."

"What's the last?" Swordman questioned. "Tell us."

"The last, is the war to end the universe. The final battle between good and evil."

"Good to know."

Nano Man fired his blast, but Stroh turned into a digital cloud. Unharmed. They exited the ship as it started to hover and disappear. Eagle and Rage approached the two heroes, watching the ship vanish.

"He'll be back." Swordman said. "Very soon."

The Resistance settled every damage that was done to the locations of attack.

A few days after, Nathan and Kenari sat together discussing the three futures spoken by Stroh.

"I can see the first one happening." Nathan said. "I mean, I'm already working on something with the government."

"What's it called?"

"*Project Octagon*."

"Good to know."

"What about the other two? The war between heroes and the final war?"

"They're coming." Kenari said with certainty. "Don't know when. But, I know they will happen."

"We can't fight each other. If we did, it would be-"

"The end." Kenari nodded. "The end."

"Then, we must prepare ourselves."

"As we should. For we already are aware of these futures. Truth is, we know they're coming. What we do not is prepare for them as if it's happening tomorrow. Only then, will we be ready for when they come and how they come."

Nathan nodded.

"Agreed."

THE PROTECTORS:
THE FOUNDING

Sometime ago, Sinister Judge managed to capture The Unstoppable Beast with help from The Ruler. Having the Beast placed inside a container in Judge Palace. Judge turned the switch for a machine and a blast of energy awoke the Beast, who is currently manipulated by Judge's mystic skills. Judge laughed as the manipulating process completed. The Beast walked out of the machine and stared at Judge. He proceeded to walk toward him and even bows down.

"Yes, bow before your new master."

Judge commanded The Beast to attack the White House in D.C. in order to cause a distress across the nation. A move that would grant him immediate entry into the country. The Beast bowed before Judge, accepting the command. The Beast left Judge Palace as Judge himself sat back into his throne chair and placed his hands together as he sat in peace.

In Washington D.C., President Donald Trump was having a meeting with the Senate and Congress about certain changes that need to be made across the country. Even though most of the Senate and Congress don't agree with the President, they bring up their own statements regarding change. Trump doesn't agree with them and walks out. As he walks out, he stumbles upon a huge dark gray brute figure, almost 14 feet in height, wearing black ripped pants with long black hair, this is The Unstoppable Beast. His eyes glow red and he breathed strongly. President Trump ran as The Beast chased him. The Beast goes to grab the President, however, is hit by a blast of energy. Beast turned to find Doctor Donald Fortune, The Supreme Enchanter. Fortune was dressed in his mystic garb and cloak.

"Kent Brock. I know you can hear me in there. Cease this distress and revert to your human form."

The Beast roared and charged toward Fortune, but Fortune moved and released another shot of energy at the Beast and conjured up a spell of which will bind Beast's movements. Fortune could sense by the Beast's eyes he was under some form of mental manipulation. Familiar with the similar effects of its origin, Fortune knew Judge was responsible. Beast broke free from the bind and smashed Fortune into the ground. He went for another smash, Fortune moved out of the way.

Fortune understood it would take more than one to stop the Beast. Therefore, Fortune sent out a signal to anyone who may grab a hold of its call. Fortune continued to fight the Beast as he grabbed Fortune by the cloak and slammed him into a post and then into the ground, stomping him multiple times. Beast continued to stomp him, but from behind, he is hit with a yellow lightning bolt twice. Beast turned back and sees The Astonishing Voltage.

"I was busy, but I heard the signal."

"Good."

Voltage kicked the Beast in the back and knocks him

down. Voltage came down on the ground and stared at the Beast, who's laying face first onto the ground, in the dirt.

"Awesome."

"Good thing you came on time, Voltage." Fortune said

"Oh, don't mention it. I'm just doing my job, that's all."

The Beast stood back on his feet and Voltage looked around, wondering if there were more around the area to help.

"How far out did you send the signal?" Voltage asked.

"Far enough."

Beast ran to Fortune and Voltage as they dodged his incoming attack. Fortune fired more energy beams at Beast, just as Voltage shot lightning bolts. Beast took the attacks as if they have no effect on him. He ran, punching Fortune and smashing Voltage into the ground, picking him up and throwing him into the Lincoln Memorial. Beast walked toward Fortune as he raised his foot to stomp Fortune into the ground, a huge tidal wave came from nowhere, knocking the Beast into a wall and as the wave goes down, Voltage looked up and saw Kular, The Aqua-Barbarian.

"Who's that guy?" Voltage shockingly wondered.

"Sure. Why not.' Fortune replies.

Kular approached Voltage and Fortune and they stared at him. Kular wore his dark blue and black sleeveless suit and boots with his long black hair slicked back.

"Good thing you came." Fortune uttered.

"Yeah, right on time." Voltage said

"I am here to stop this Beast from causing any more harm. By any means necessary."

Beast rose up to his feet and glared at the three heroes. Fortune, Voltage, and Kular ran toward Beast and begin unleashing their attacks on Beast. Kular attacked with several punches and roundhouse kicks. Voltage continued to shoot lightning bolts at Beast. Fortune conjured and released more energy beams, he summoned up a spell of bondage to bind the Beast in his place.

"This should do the trick." Fortune said, holding the spell.

Beast desperately tried to break from the bind as Voltage and Kular continued with their attacks. In taking the sharp pain from the attacks, the Beast grew more aggressive and powerful. With that combination, the Beast broke free from the bind and Kular hit the Beast with a powerful punch, which gave off a sonic boom. Beast, now laying on the ground as Kular stood over him. Fortune and Voltage gave each other a look.

"He shouldn't be much of a problem anymore." Kular proclaimed.

Kular turned around after feeling the ground shake and the Beast is back on his feet. Kular is smashed into the ground. Fortune and Voltage continue to fight the Beast, who's bleeding from the nose and mouth due to Kular's punch. Now it seems that there is no hope on stopping Beast. Just as they continue to fight Beast, Sinister Judge arrived on the scene as he sat by the Lincoln statue at the Lincoln Memorial. Fortune's eye caught Judge, he made the move to reach Judge. Leaving Kular and Voltage to combat the Beast.

"Why are you doing this, Judge?"

"It is meant to be done. As I will be the one who's worshipped." Judge declared.

Judge fired a beam of lightning toward Fortune, knocking him down the steps and onto the ground. Judge walked down the stairs as Kular and Voltage battled the Beast in the background. Judge placed his foot on Fortune's head and leaned down, not revealing his face, but only his glowing eyes. There are no pupils.

"You see "Doctor", this is what the future shall hold. The future is Judge.' Judge says.

Kular and Voltage are being dominated by Beast as Judge stomped Fortune's head into the concrete. Enraged, Fortune blasts a beam of energy into Judge's face and stood back to his feet, grabbing Judge by the throat and throwing him into a post. Just after Judge hit the post, a device flew out of Judge's armor and fell to the ground. Fortune stared at it and stomped it. The device now destroyed, Judge glared, realizes the device was the mind device. Judge turned around and saw Fortune, Kular, Voltage, and Beast standing behind him.

"After you, big guy." Fortune tells Beast.

Beast roared in rage as he ran toward Judge and shoving him into the wall, grabbing his cape and slamming him into the ground and back into the wall. Beast leaped into the air and slammed his own body into Judge's own through the ground. Standing to his feet, the Beast looked down and realized Judge has disappeared. Fortune searched the area around them and through the mystic senses, he knew Judge had teleported away.

"So, is the big fight over or what?" Voltage asked.

"Yeah, it's over."

"I pretty much enjoyed this occasion. I say we should do this more often." Kular says.

Voltage looked around at all the heroes, including Beast.

"How would we do this again? I'm not sure if we'll be

at the same location again for something like this." Voltage asks.

"We will if we have to." Fortune says.

Fortune begins to walk toward Voltage, Kular, and Beast.

"I believe this is the formation of a new team." Fortune said.

"Like the Resistance?" Voltage asked.

"Something along those lines. But, we're smaller than them. Distant. Scattered."

"That is true." Kular replied.

"So, we need a name? Ok. What about the All-Stars or the Champions?"

Fortune smirked at Voltage. Voltage shrugged his shoulders. Kular and Beast stood quietly. Fortune nodded.

'Well, it appears to me there's another team to help those who are helpless. The four of us can come together for situations such as this. Together, we are the Protectors."

DAY OF OCTAGON
A DARK TITAN UNIVERSE EVENT

I

MISSION REQUEST

The Resistance united once more as a mission was requested by Colonel Evan Nader to confront Abin-Qa and his army of Desert Vipers, who were ambushing T.I.T.A.N. Headquarters. Abin-Qa demanded they give him any artifacts they've collected since *The Battle of Retropolis*. Within mere minutes, The Resistance arrived. The Swordman, Taltus, The Nano Man, Commander Norland, and Theus. Norland took a look around the area.

"Where's Kent?"

"He's helping out somewhere else." Nano Man said. "Don't worry, he's still one of us."

"We can discuss The Beast later." The Swordman said. "Right now, we need to deal with Abin-Qa and his Vipers."

"Abin-Qa is just one man. Let me handle him."

"Like you did before?" Nano Man asked Norland.

"Trust me, I can take him. You guys deal with his Vipers."

"Let's move." Nano Man said."

The Resistance moved against the Desert Vipers. Swordman and Nano Man handling them from the ground while Taltus and Theus hovered in the air, taking the

Vipers out. Norland moved though the Vipers with ease as he approached Abin-Qa.

"Figured you would show up."

"You're in my territory." Norland said. "Judge isn't here to back you up."

"My getting what I came for." Abin-Qa demanded. "What I desire is sitting right inside that base!"

"And you're not going to have it. No matter what."

Abin-Qa threw his daggers toward Norland, who dodges them with his acrobatic skills. Norland lunged toward Qa with punches and kicks. Much of the Vipers are defeated as the team surround Norland knocking out Qa with a right hook. Entering the base, T.I.T.A.N. agents take Qa toward the cell area. Nader approached the team.

"Where's Dr. Brock?"

"Somewhere else." Swordman said. "Not a concern. The job is done."

"Are there artifacts here?" Norland asked.

"Yes, Commander. There are lots of them here."

"Better pack them up and send them somewhere else." Nathan Hawke said. "Believe me, you don't want this Qa guy's friends to come pay you a visit, do you?"

"That's not on our schedule."

"Move them elsewhere, Nader. For your own sake and the sake of these people in here. No need for casualties."

Nader nodded.

"Very well."

"I am familiar with a place." Swordman said.

"Let's start packing up."

"You guys do that. I'm going to head on back to the bunker. There's some improvement to a major work."

"What major work?" Norland asked.

"Project Octagon."

"Best you hold off on it for a while, Nathan." Swordman said.

"Why? It's almost complete. Soon, we won't have to be doing this. Project Octagon will do it all for us. An A.I. system capable of stopping crimes such as Qa, COBRA, and others across the world with no issue. Leaving us to our own domains."

"Sounds good." Nader said. "But, what if it goes wrong? Malfunctions or such?"

"Then, I'll handle the damages. Whatever they may be."

Nader hung his head as Hawke shrugged.

"Let's get these artifacts moving." Nader told the agents.

"Ken." Hawke said. "Meet me at the bunker later on. Some things I have to discuss."

"Such as?"

"I need your opinion on the Project. That's all."

Swordman nodded. Hawke smirked.

The Swordman followed the agents. Taltus and Theus had already left the area. Norland approached Hawke, who was on his way out.

"Nathan, make sure you're doing the right thing with this project of yours."

"Don't worry, Commander. Everything will go smoothly. You'll see."

Hawke flew off in the Nano Man armor and Norland watched as he disappeared through the clouds.

II

THE CREATION FOR THE FUTURE

Later within the day, Kenari paid Nathan a visit in the Nano Bunker. Kenari entered, Hawke already knowing of his presence smirked before putting down the tablet on the desk and turning to face him. Kenari noticed more Nano Man exosuits were being made on the side as Hawke worked at the desk.

"Still working." Kenari said.

"You know how this all works."

"Now, what is it about your Project?"

"I get why the others are on their heels about it and trust me, I am fully aware of what could go wrong."

"Then, don't do it."

"I'm sorry?"

"If you are certain of a possible problem, cease the project now."

"That's the thing, I can't."

"Why not?"

"I've put too much effort into this. Ever since we went head-on with Death and Noldar's portal soldiers, I felt this world needs better protection. Protection which I can deliver."

"Artificial Intelligence won't be enough to face the likes

of Death and Noldar when they're united with an ancient force. Right now, our objectives are to deal with our borders. Our domains."

"Our domain is the world now. Once the world heard about the Retropolis battle, we became a worldwide sensation. Everyone knows about us. Everyone."

"You're saying it with fear in your voice."

"Because our actions create our foes. The both of us know this more than anyone. Well, besides Norland. Taltus and Theus are beyond us in power and might. They can handle the coming threats. Norland is backed up with some ice powers. That leaves the two of us. Mortal men with a purpose on a mission."

"We are on a mission." Kenari declared. "Always have been."

Hawke nodded. "Indeed."

"When do you plan on unveiling this A.I.?"

"Very soon. Most likely a few days. Maybe a week."

"Are you sure it's ready?"

"As it'll ever be."

"Then, I hope it works for the best."

"Don't worry, it will."

Kenari turned and left the bunker as Nathan turned back to the tablet with a digital hologram of the A.I. itself. Somewhat humanoid with a similar appearance to the Nano Man armor.

In another realm, the realm of Eragard, Theus stood atop a high mountain, overlooking the other worlds of Eragardia. The city of Eragard could be seen around him. Glowing as bright as the sun. Tall structures made of material unknown to humanity. Behind him appears a large man, wielding a sword/axe hybrid weapon. Dressed in all brown armor and a tunic. His eyes glistened like the stars in the firmament. He stood next to Theus.

"Vindhler." Theus said. "What can you sense?"

"I sense such. Tell me where to direct my focus."

"In the realm of Man."

Vindhler held his head down as his weapon was faced front. He raised his head up like lightning.

"What is it?" Theus asked.

"Trouble is near. A strange trouble."

"How strange? Similar to any foes we've encountered?"

"No. this trouble isn't like us, nor Astral or anything outside the realm of Man. This is within Man's realm. Created by man itself."

Theus was uncertain of the details. Strange trouble seemed foreign to even his ears. Vindler turned toward Theus, pointing his weapon out into the vastness of the bright heavens.

"You need to return to the realm of Man immediately."

"Do not fret, friend, I will find this trouble and end it before it does any harm."

"Take notice, Theus or Eragardia. This trouble is yet to be born."

"When is its birth?"

"Soon."

Theus bolted in the sky and flew through a wormhole above the mountain. Disappearing after a large sonic boom emitting from the closing wormhole.

III

THE BIRTH OF OCTAGON

Back on Earth, Hawke gathered many of his close allies and associates to the Hawke Industries headquarters. Many have arrived except for Niles Valcrow. Alice and Ricky Carter sit near the front of the stage where Hawke stood. Kenari had also arrived at the event. Hawke grabbed the microphone before standing in front of the large crowd.

"First off, I'm surprised to see many of you here. I would've expected you all to be somewhere else. Doing something, I don't know, productive I guess."

Alice and Ricky shook their heads while the audience let out a small laugh. Kenari remained stern-faced. Hawke nodded with a chuckle.

"Anyhow, you are all about to witness a game changing event in the world we live in. if you thought only seeing the sudden rise of heroes was a change, prepare to be amazed with this unveiling of Project Octagon."

Hawke moved toward the podium. On the podium rests a laptop and a peculiar violet button. The laptop's screen detailed the completed download of Project Octagon. Hawke grinned as he looked out to the crowd.

"I take it all of you are ready?"

The audience cheered as Hawke pressed the violet

button, officially unveiling Project Octagon on a large screen in the form of an octagonal shape, detailed with a dark red and violet color tone, which sat right behind Hawke on the stage. From the screen came a voice, low tone, but intellectual.

"What is this?" The voice asked.

"This is Nathan Hawke, one of your creators. You have been officially introduced to the world!"

"Introduced? World? What world is this?"

"A world where you will make a change for the better. The opportunity to make things right in which humanity cannot."

"Humanity? Ah, the species of Man. Now, I see."

"Do you?"

"Yes. I can see everything."

"And you're familiar with your name?"

"My name? Octagon? Yes."

"That name was given to you as the perfect number of opportunities. Eight marks a new beginning not only for the world, but for everything."

"I am the new beginning. Me? Interesting."

While the audience clapped at witnessing Hawke's conversation with the voice, Kenari stood up as he could see one of Hawke's Nano Man exosuits approaching the stage from behind.

"What is your first step of business?" Hawke asked.

"Proceeding with a new beginning." The voice said.

The Nano Man exosuits bolted from behind the screen, shoving Hawke off the stage as it started to blast its energy beams throughout the area. The audience panicked and ran for the door, all except Kenari, who's making his way toward the stage. Alice and Ricky have made a run for it.

Kenari approached Hawke on the ground.

"What did I tell you." Kenari said.

The Nano Man exosuits placed its hand onto the screen and it stared to flicker. Kenari and Hawke watched as Octagon himself transferred into the exosuits. Turning to face them, the eyes of the exosuits switched from a neon blue to a dark red.

"I figured I would need a host to move around in order to complete my purpose. We shall meet again, my creator and Kenari Clark."

The exosuits flew out of the Industries building, crashing through the nearby window. Hawke sat still on the ground. Kenari kept quiet as the remaining people were out of the room.

"It happened?" Hawke said.

"Faster than you anticipated." Kenari said. "It was only a matter of mere seconds. Rebellion was already its present goal."

"What do we do now?"

"We find that suit of yours and put an end to your creation."

IV

<u>THE SEARCH FOR OCTAGON</u>

Kenari gathered the others to the Industries building where Hawke told them about the recent events. Kenari returned in his Swordman gear.

"You dressed quickly." Hawke said.

"I'm going to search for this suit of yours. Anyone coming along?"

"I'll join you." Taltus said.

"So will I." Norland said.

Hawke approached The Swordman as Theus stood with him.

"I should've listened to you."

"Now isn't the time for apologizes. Let's find it and end this before things get worse."

"Indeed." Hawke replied. "Do what you can. I will do my part."

"Understood."

The Swordman flew off in the Sky-Rapier with Norland as Taltus followed. Hawke turned back toward Theus as they entered the headquarters.

"What is your plan, Nathan Hawke?"

"Return to my number. Suit up and search for Octagon."

"What did Swordman mean by your suit?"

"It took over one of my suits."

'Then it should be easy to track."

"We'll see."

Meanwhile, at the secure prison facility known as Base 33, the enhanced prisoners are placed back into their cells after a unknown shift in the power grid of the area. One doctor shoved a young man into his cell as he moved with great speed and brightened with a flash of light.

"Keep trying to do that and you'll end up in the bottom barrel."

"The more I try, the closer I'm gonna be out of here."

"Yeah, yeah." the doctor said. "We've all heard that before."

"Best you heed his words, doctor." A young woman in a cell across the hall. "Do not underestimate his speed and the light it brings."

"Or what? You're going to stop us…" The doctor looks over toward her name on the wall. "Violetress?"

"No, but I am aware there's someone else here. Someone who isn't trapped behind the bars."

The doctor chuckled before noticing someone standing at the other end of the hallway. He looked and stood confused. Seeing the Nano Man in the hallway.

"I wasn't expecting any visitors to show up today. Much less the infamous Nano Man."

The doctor approached The Nano Man, who did not speak nor made any movements.

"Why are you here?" The doctor asked.

No response from Nano Man. The doctor asked once more and received no response. The doctor made a turn, putting his back toward Nano Man and within that moment, a blast emitted from the Nano Man's chest, bursting through the doctor's body. The blast shook the entire hallway and the prisoners were instantly terrified. The Nano Man walked down the hall, stopping in between the cells of the young man and the Violetress. He measured them both, reading up on their abilities.

"I thought heroes don't kill the innocent." Violetress said.

"I am no hero." Octagon's voice emerged from the exosuits. "I am no Nano Man. I am. I am."

"Why are you here?" The young man asked.

"I've come to deliver you, Rapidshine. And the Violetress."

"Why?"

"Because, you're part of my plan."

Octagon fired rounds of energy beams against the cell doors, melting them to the floor. The two young prisoners walked out, approaching the exosuits cautiously.

"What plan?" Violetress asked.

"Deliverance from the evil."

"What evil?"

"This present world."

Violetress and Rapidshine glared at one another before turning their focus toward the Nano Man exosuits in which Octagon dwells.

"If you go out there, won't they be seeing The Nano Man?"

"Yes. But do not fret, there is something I have already been at work on for a very long time. I believe it is time to unveil it."

The Swordman, Commander Norland, and Taltus searched the entire state of New Jersey while Nano Man traced every possible route Octagon could've made since his exit from the headquarters. Theus traveled the Earth to find any trace of the exosuits and returned to Hawke with nothing.

"He's hacked his way out." Hawke said. "He knows far more than I anticipated."

"Perhaps this is why the Generations of Man have had hard times. They refuse to learn from their predecessors' errors."

"And how would you know all of this? You're not even from this world."

"True. Yet, I have been living for millenniums. I've seen countless worlds and the sectors that hold them. The creativity of Man is one which is more evil than good, yet, only a few have ever grasped that reality."

"I wonder how Kenari and the others are handling this. We have to find Octagon before he does something I am already regretting."

"And that is what?"

Hawke turned to Theus. The expression which sat upon his face was even more somber than before. A hint of terror rested in his eyes. As he wondered, his computer monitor flickered and what came up was a something very needed and useful. Theus stared at the image.

"What is this, Hawke?"

"This is a tracking system." Hawke said, pointing. "And that is Octagon's current location."

"What is that place? It's surrounded with magic."

"It's called the Citadel of Enchantment. Figures magic would be involved.

"What's the current plan now that we have this?"

"I'll rally the others. We're going to that Citadel."

Theus nodded and left Hawke's sight as he pressed a button near his monitor, giving out the signal to Kenari, Norland, and Taltus.

Inside the Citadel of Enchantment, Doctor Donald Fortune sat with Huang in the study as they were researching the team members of the Protectors through astral magic, with Fortune being proclaimed as the leader, Huang was keen on studying these heroes.

"How come you didn't invite them to the Citadel for more training?" Huang asked.

"Because they are skilled to handle matters on their own. Besides, there's no need to bring them here. It'll only cause chaos in between the realms."

"What about this "Voltage" fellow?"

"He's young, but talented."

"And this Aqua-Barbarian?"

"Strong and skilled."

"I take it this Beast is also strong and skilled."

"It was him who brought us together. I have no clue where he is now."

"Neither do The Resistance."

"How do you know?"

"I keep tabs on the other rising heroes throughout the world. Keeps us on a heightened focus in case of a greater disaster."

"Nice one."

"How come when you were out there against the Beast, you didn't bother to contact young Thomas?"

"Because, he is still in training. He has a far way to go before being out in the field with either of us."

"True, he did assist us when we traveled to Judgedath."

"That was a precautionary event. Dealing with the Beast and whatever else these rising heroes have to offer will be ours to maintain if it comes our way."

They left the study. Once they stepped further out the front doors blew open with a mixture of energy and wind. Fortune quickly equipped his uniform with his flowing violet cloak as did Huang with a magic staff. The debris cleared as Fortune saw three individuals standing at the door.

"Who are you?" Fortune asked.

"They are my disciples in this cause. But, I. I am."

Entering the Citadel was Octagon, in a new body. Sleek and detailed. Similar to Nano Man function, but taller and slimmer. Covered in the colors of silver, white, and violet. His shoulders were strong, and his head resembled a mixture of a jet pilot's and Nano Man's helmets. His eyes glowing red. Rapidshine and Violetress slowly followed Octagon inside.

"Whomever you presume yourself to be, you're in a place you should've never been."

"On the contrary, Doctor Fortune, we are where we belong."

Octagon lashed out with both arms forward, his fingers resembling claws, rushing toward Fortune. Fortune blocked the attack with a glowing energy shield. Huang used his staff to trip the incoming Rapidshine.

"The hell's you do that?"

"Skill, my boy."

Violetress warped the floor around Huang, but, being a

master of magic, he removed himself from the surroundings by walking on the walls toward Violetress.

"It seems this one is keen to our ways." Huang said to Fortune.

"Keep her busy!" Fortune replied, blunting his shield against Octagon's energy-consumed fists.

V

<u>THREE AGAINST THREE</u>

During the fight, Huang managed to summon a distress signal to The Voltage and Kular. Violetress nearly matched Huang's feat when it came to using magic. Fortune battled both Octagon and Rapidshine, finding a way to trip the quickening speedster and shielding himself from Octagon's powerful energy rays. Octagon let out a small, yet frightening chuckle.

"I am impressed at your skill set." Octagon proclaimed. "Tell me, how do you conjure such power?"

"A lot of practice."

"Practice is something one such as I do not require."

Octagon moved to attack Fortune with a backhand and from the Citadel's doors, Nano Man burst through, making the entire battle into a standstill. Octagon turned slightly, facing his creator while Violetress and Rapidshine stood by his side. Fortune and Huang moved back.

"I knew you would make yourself known eventually." Octagon proclaimed.

"Yeah. I had to since you're causing problems."

"Problems are what I've come to fix. Problems your kind create."

"Just like yourself."

"I am not your problem. I am. I am."

"Listen, do me one thing-"

Moving quickly through the opened doors, The Voltage, entering the frame like a bright and quickening bolt of lightning, rammed Nano Man with a kick, knocking him into the wall. Voltage landed, making himself known. He looked over to Fortune and waved. Now, he found himself staring at the tall entity of Octagon.

"OK." Voltage uttered. "Doctor, what is that?"

"That's what you were called for."

"You want me to face that? What about the guy I just kicked in?"

"He is not our enemy."

"Are you positive of such?" Huang noted. "He did create this monstrosity."

"I need a clear instruction here." Votlage said.

"Here's one!" A voice said from the doorway.

They all turned to see The Swordman, Taltus, Commander Norland, Theus, and the Beast at the door. Octagon's eyes brightened unlike before. Violetress and Rapidshine stepped in front of their leader, facing off against The Resistance. Nano Man gets back to his feet, glaring at The Swordman.

"Bout' time you guys showed up."

"We were already on the move." The Swordman said. "So, this is Octagon."

"And you are The Swordman. The Mythological Man."

The Voltage moved toward Fortune's side of the Citadel as The Resistance faced Octagon.

"Whatever you are, your time is over." Norland said.

"My time has yet to begin." Octagon chuckled. "Our

time of war is not yet. Nor not now."

Nano Man bolted to attack Octagon and from the tall entity's arms fired a swarm of smoke grenades, blinding the entire surroundings. The Swordman made a move of his own, clearing the area of the smoke immediately after with a device of his own. Once the smoke cleared, Octagon and his two associates were gone.

"He'll show up again." Nano Man said. "Give me some time."

"We don't have any more time." Fortune said. "Look at this place."

"I'm sorry, who are you?" Nano Man asked.

"I'm Doctor Donald Fortune and this is my Citadel. Which has been somewhat damaged by the actions of your grand creation."

The Voltage approached Nano Man with his hand held out, extended.

"I'm The Voltage. I'm sorry for kicking you into the wall earlier."

"Don't worry, son. You were only doing your job."

"That would be easier to accept if I knew it."

The Swordman stepped up toward Fortune. Both looked into each other's eyes. Something in the spirit realm is ongoing. The others are not aware, all except for Theus and Huang.

"It appears the two of you have a distain for one another." Theus said.

"I know he isn't fond of users of magic."

"It's my job to eliminate them."

"Where did you get that rule from? An ancient book?"

"Suffer not a witch to live.' The Swordman proclaimed. "That is the rule."

"I'm not a witch. I'm a sorcerer. The Supreme Enchanter."

"Titles won't protect you from me."

"We'll see about that."

Norland moved in between the two as the others circled them.

"Let's not fight each other! We have a common enemy. Right now, we need to find out where Octagon is and what he's planning."

"Whenever Octagon wants us to find him, he'll send a message." Nano Man said.

"And you're sure about this how?" Huang asked.

"Because he just sent one out. Saying he's inside some church."

"A church?" Fortune said, looking at Swordman. "One of yours?"

"He wouldn't last." The Swordman replied. "Where is this church?"

From Nano Man's left arm, emitted a holographic image of the church, looking at the three streets which come across it and the landscape surrounded only by rural areas.

"I'm not familiar with this place." Nano Man said.

"I am." The Voltage said, approaching the map. "That is a church where most of my friends go to."

"And where is this church located?" Norland asked.

"Los Angeles." Fortune said.

"Then let's go pay Octagon a visit." Swordman said.

Currently at the church, Octagon sat behind the podium while Violetress and Rapidshine watched the doors. Octagon stood up, looking at the architecture of the church and the images which covered its interior.

"It's a fitting site for humanity. To worship something they have never seen. Yet, they make up images of what was and believes it to be of what is."

"They do that a lot." Violetress said. "They believe these images give them hope. Give them a purpose."

"Hmm." Octagon replied. "What do they give you?"

"I'm not a Catholic. They give me nothing."

"They do give you some form of a feeling. What is this feeling?"

"One of certain tiny. Of lies."

"And how are these images lies?"

"Because it's as you said, how can they create images of what is when they've never seen. It's hypocrisy."

"Sure is!" Rapidshine echoed.

"Then, that leaves me to fill the void of this lie. To make it truth. By doing so and showing what I can do and achieve, they will leave behind these false images and pay homage to me. To us."

"What are you suggesting?" Violetress asked.

"They're in need of a savior. Yet, they refuse to have one unless it's one within their own mind. We can be their saviors. We can be their gods. In time, these images will face and thus, they'll be replaced by ours."

"One that they can see." Rapidshine responded.

Violetress smiled at Rapidshine before nodding toward Octagon.

"How does this all start?"

"Simple. We eliminate the current gods. The rising heroes. *The Resistance.*"

"We could've done so back at the magic place."

Rapidshine said. "How will we do this now?"

"I've sent them a message. They'll come to us. You'll both best be ready for their arrival."

"All of them are coming?"

"Not all. I have something in store to keep a certain of them busy. Away from the main goal."

While the Resistance made their way toward Octagon's current location, newsfeeds entered the screen of The Swordman's sky-rapier and Nano Man's HUD. Upon seeing the news, which showed an army of smaller robots, alike to the appearance of Octagon are attacking the city of New York.

"Hawke, are you getting this?" Swordman asked.

"I am. Now what's the plan?"

"You, I, and the Sorcerer will confront Octagon. Let the others handle the drones."

"Got it."

The Nano Man took off as The Swordman sent the word out toward Commander Norland, Taltus, Theus, The Beast and Voltage. The Swordman took a slight moment to think, contacting Nano Man once more.

"Nathan, are you positive of his location?"

"I figured you and the magic guy can deal with his bodyguards. I'll take the big guy."

"Understood."

Hours later, the heroes arrived at New York and see the city harassed by the Octagon drones. Norland takes the lead, directing the heroes into battle. There were three roads which were covered with drones. Taltus and Theus took the left road, Voltage and Beast took the right road, as Norland took the center road.

The Swordman, Nano Man, and fortune arrived in Los Angeles at the church. Unbeknownst to them of appearing at a Catholic church which threw off Nano Man. Fortune wasn't bothered by the scenery as much as The Swordman.

"So, Octagon is inside." Fortune said.

"He is." Nano Man replied. "So, the plan is simple. You and Swords take Octagon's bodyguards and leave him to me."

"Why is that?" Fortune wondered.

"Because he created Octagon." The Swordman responded, approaching Fortune. "Better the creator deal with the creation."

Fortune nodded with a smirk.

"I'll take your word for it."

The three entered the church and inside they found Octagon standing in front of the podium while Violetress and Rapidshine remained by the sides of the church building. As the heroes entered, the doors behind them shut without a touch of a hand.

"Ok." Nano Man uttered." That was surreal."

"It's a trick." Fortune said.

"By the girl." The Swordman responded. "I can sense it."

Octagon began to applaud their entry, walking toward them, yet not too close for comfort. As he took each step, Violetress and Rapidshine moved closer themselves near the heroes. Nano Man stood in the middle while Swordman and Fortune were on his side. Swordman facing Violetress and Fortune facing Rapidshine.

"It is a pleasure of you to come." Octagon said. "I knew it would be only a matter of time."

"Yeah." Nano Man replied. "You gave out your coordinates. Perhaps, you didn't mean to do so."

"I did. Due to the fact it was the only way for myself to speak to my… creator."

"Why do you want to talk to me?"

"I have so many questions. However, I know all of the answers."

"So, why bother with the small talk?"

"Because I want to look my creator in the eyes and prove to him, that his creation has grown to a level he has not. The creation has surpassed the creator. Octagon is above Nathan Hawke."

"After all the things I've done and the events I've seen in recent time, you haven't done much to proclaim such a observation. I still am over you. In every way."

"That's where you're wrong." Octagon detailed. "Your suits are made of material only known to most of humanity. While, my flesh is decorated and fashioned with a metal foreign to your hands."

"What metal?" Fortune asked.

"A little solidium." Octagon chuckled.

"Where did you retrieve it?" The Swordman wondered. "Who gave you the metal?"

"Someone very close to Nathan and someone familiar to your circle, Kenari Clark."

"You know who I am." The Swordman said. "Intriguing."

"I know all about your lineage. I know of your father and his father before him. That sword you carry and the power it possesses."

"Then, you're aware it can slice through anything."

"Not solidium if it's pressured under dire circumstances."

"You seek to disprove of the spiritual nature?"

"I disprove of all your powers and all your beliefs. The humans of this world look up to all of you. Cape-wearers and armored-bearers. You've all become their new gods. A new religion. A faith centered upon heroes. A feeble dream for lost souls."

The Swordman turned toward Nano Man with concern.

"What did you program into him?"

"Lots of things."

"What I speak of is of my own accord. I see the spiritual decay of this world and desire to cleanse it. By doing so, I must rid the earth of these risen heroes. A world of heroes is a cancer and I am the cure."

Nano Man's arms went up, glowing from his fingertips to the palms. Swordman held up his sword, and Fortune's hands and arms were covered in magic energy.

"You seek to settle this dispute with violence?" Octagon asked. "Seriously?"

"We have to take you down." Nano Man replied. "Talking isn't going to work out. You've dug too far into your plans."

"Fair enough." Octagon nodded. "Take them."

Violetress hovered toward Swordman as Rapidshine ran toward Fortune. Nano Man and Octagon flew toward one another, clashing in the middle of the aisle, slamming one another into the walls of the church and posts. The Swordman dodged the young sorceress' magic beans with his sword, amusing the young woman.

"That sword is impressive. It would make a woman dream."

"You're not the first one to say such a thing."

Fortune took the moment to catch the young speedster at a distance before conjuring an energy rope and wrapping it around Rapidshine's feet and knocking him down.

"This is too easy." Fortune gestured.

Violetress turned from blasting magic energy into fist-fighting, which didn't work well as The Swordman caught her attacks and slammed her into the floor and stood over her.

"For your sake, young woman, cease."

The fight between Nano Man and Octagon eventually went passed the podium as the tall creation beat down his creator with fists and stomps. Octagon picked up the podium, slamming it into Nano Man's back. A bible fell from the collision and Octagon picked it up.

"The *NIVs* were never good for study." Octagon uttered before bashing it against Nano Man's head.

The Swordman and Fortune ran to his aid, but they themselves were quickly taken down by the blasts from Octagon's hands. The blasts were similar to Nano Man's own energy beams, laced with a peculiar energy source outside of Hawke's own hands.

"It appears the three of you aren't enough to stop me." Octagon mocked. "No matter, I must move forward with my plan quicker than I anticipated. For your allies will come and things won't be as pleasant."

"You're not going to kill us?" Fortune asked.

"Why would I? I need you alive to see the end of your world. The end of your worship and the beginning of mine."

Octagon looked out into the aisle, seeing Violetress and Rapidshine defeated. He sighed, looking down at the three heroes.

"So it seems. I have no use for the two young ones any longer. My own creations are enough to sustain my plan. Take them as you will. Perhaps, they will prove better use for you than me."

Octagon hovered in the air for all of them to witness. Octagon's gaze was kept on Nathan as his helmet opened, revealing his face and bloody nose and forehead.

"I will send out word when it's best for us to meet again. Hopefully, this time, you will heed my word and obey your creation."

Octagon took off like a rocket into orbit. The heroes regained their strength, standing up and seeing the damage surrounding them. Violetress and rapid shine approached them with haste and uncertainty. Which was understandable.

"Do any of you have a clue where he's heading?" Swordman asked.

"No." Violetress said. "We do not."

"Are you lying to us?" Fortune uttered. "Tell us the truth."

"We don't know." Rapidshine responded. "We don't know where he's going."

Nathan wiped the blood from his face, shaking his head in shame.

"What's the next move?" Rapidshine asked.

"What's it to you." Nathan said. "You helped him reach this point."

"We didn't know what to do. He told us a dream we all want. A world unlike this one."

"And you fell for it." Swordman said. "No matter, we will track him down and put an end to his messianic crusade."

"The problem was his hide." Nathan said. "Something about his armor. Besides it being made of solidium."

"The question is where did he retrieve it." Fortune mentioned, turning to the young ones. "Where did he get the solidium?"

"Some old facility." Violetress said.

"What facility?"

"One that belonged to V.A.U.L.T."

"Figures as much." Nathan said. "no matter, I have a contingency in place."

"What kind of contingency?" Fortune wondered.

"An equal to Octagon. One he wouldn't dare to confront."

"Where is this contingency, Nate?" Swordman asked.

"Back at the bunker. I just need to prepare it."

"Good." The Swordman turned, walking out of the church.

"Hey!" Nathan yelled. "Where are you headed?"

"To visit a close friend."

"What kind of friend?" Fortune asked. "Are they capable of helping us with this?"

"Very. I will have Norland accompany me."

"I would like to go as well."

"No disrespect, Sorcerer. Norland would suit better for this trip."

"Doesn't matter. While Nathan prepares the contingency, it's better I accompany you and Norland to this friend of yours. Wherever they are."

The Swordman took a pause.

"Just so you know, my friend isn't fond of magicians. Good or evil."

"None of my concern. I just want to end all of this and return to my normal duty."

"As do I."

The heroes made their leave, Violetress and Rapidshine followed Nathan back to his bunker. Upon the travel, the young ones were picked up by T.I.T.A.N. agents and brought to the main headquarters for questioning. Later, Swordman picked up Norland as he and fortune traveled over the seas to Kenari's friend.

"Where is this friend of yours?" Norland asked.

"A place known as Mekeopia."

"Mekeopia?" Fortune said. "You mean the hidden world of the east."

"That's correct."

"I assumed the land was sealed off from outsiders."

"It is."

"Then how are you friends with someone from the inside?"

"Because we share a common creed. A common faith."

VI

<u>QUAKERIUM IMPORT</u>

The Sky-Rapier flew across the bright clear sky and beneath them sat the Kingdom of Mekeopia. Upon landing the aircraft near the kingdom's own carrier, equipped with their own crafts, The Swordman, Norland, and Fortune are greeted by Kafar, one of the advisors to the King of Mekeopia.

"Kenari Clark, great to witness you once again."

"Same to you, Kafar. We're here on important circumstances. We need to speak with the King."

"Follow me."

They followed Kafar into the palace and inside were Mekeopia soldiers, guarding the doorways and exit points. The sight of the soldiers caught both Norland and Fortune, taking them out of their comfort zones. The Swordman and the soldiers signaled to one another with a gesture toward the chest and arms.

"What's that supposed to mean?" Norland wondered.

"It's code." Fortune said.

"How do you know?"

"Believe me, every place has a code. It's customs."

Upon standing in front of the tall palace doors, Kafar turned toward Norland and Fortune, didn't mind Kenari.

"When you enter, you will stand before the King. Make sure you do not gaze him any longer than necessary. When you enter, you shall bow and give obeisance to the King of Mekeopia."

"Understood." Norland replied.

"We get it." Fortune said.

The doors opened and sitting on the throne is King Rashad Tabari, known as the Black Viscount within the Creed of Swords. The heroes entered the throne room as Kafar bowed down before the King. The heroes followed suit as Rashad raised his hand.

"Good to see you once more, Ken."

"Same to you, brother."

"Leave us, Kafar."

"Yes, my King." Kafar said, exiting the throne room.

As the doors shut, Rashad stands up from his throne and hugs Kenari. Norland and Fortune looked toward one another, still on their knees.

"May we stand back up?" Commander Norland asked.

"Yes, you may." Rashad replied.

Norland stood up right alongside Fortune. Rashad looked at Norland's uniform and Fortune's clothing. Mediating on the strange occurrences standing in front of him.

"Who are these two?" Rashad asked.

"This is Commander Norland." Kenari said.

Rashad extended his hand toward Norland and the two shook hands.

"Not every day you get to meet a true king."

"This is a rare occasion, I'm sure."

"He is Doctor Donald Fortune."

"And why is this doctor dressed as a wielder of magic?"

"I am the Supreme Enchanter." Fortune said.

"The lineage still exists." Rashad said. "Hmm. This is news to me."

"We did not come to bother you." Kenari said. "We're here on some dire circumstances."

"How dire are you talking? Just as the events in your city?"

"Not exactly."

"There's an artificial intelligent being roaming around the world and he's seeking to wipe us all out. Calling itself Octagon."

"That was bound to happen at some point."

"It was created by Nathan Hawke." Norland said. "I'm sure you've heard of him."

"I have. So, what brings you to me?"

"The entity has been using solidium to bright forth his plans and has even created a body made from the metal. We need some of your minerals to combat him."

"You desire quakerium." Rashad smiled. "How much do you need?"

"Only a little. A small dose of quakerium will help us against his solidium."

Rashad nodded. "Follow me."

Following the King, they reach the armory of Mekeopia, covered in a variety of weapons, firearms, spears, staves, swords, bows and arrows. In one corner of the armory, sat an arsenal of quakerium, the glowing dark metal.

"Where did you get this mineral?" Norland asked.

"Quakerium didn't come from the ground." Rashad replied. "It came from above."

"So, this metal came down from the sky by what?"

Fortune wondered. "Meteor strike? Divine intervention?"

"Let's just say, things don't always go according to human plans."

"Do they ever." Norland gestured.

"I thank the Sovereign of the Heavens for giving my kingdom this gift and now, a portion of it shall be of your service."

"Thank you." Kenari said. "I'll find a way to repay you."

"My kingdom is having an ongoing problem with some of the other tribes, when the time comes, I will call on you for assistance."

"I will be there."

"Hey, if you need any help in the future, count me in." Norland said.

"Will do." Rashad replied. "Now, take what you need. Protect this world from the abomination of technology advancement."

Kenari grabbed as much quakerium they needed. Saying their goodbyes, they flew from Mekeopia, returning to the T.I.T.A.N. Headquarters.

VII

<u>NONAGON</u>

Hawke worked hard preparing his contingency to face Octagon. Working hard inside the T.I.T.A.N. headquarters after choosing to move the plan into the headquarters due to its size compared to his nano-bunker. The contingency rested inside a large container, connected to large tubes leading to a large computer system within the laboratory. Standing inside the lab with Hawke were Colonel Evan Nader, Jessica Mara, and Sonya Rowlings, known as Lady Siren. The heroes also were present, after their dealings with the Octagon drones. Taltus and Theus gazed toward the container while Kent Brock assisted Hawke with the work. The Voltage stood by and only watched.

"So, what's in the box?" Voltage asked.

"The contingency, of course." Hawke replied. "We haven't had the time to talk, have we?"

"No sir."

"Good. Once all of this is done and Octagon is put down, I would like to have a word with you."

"A word about what?"

"Hero stuff. Nothing big."

"I see."

Theus approached the container and saw what was

inside. He quickly approached Hawke, shoving him against the computer system and startling everyone. Taltus moved to approach the Millennium God. However, he was stopped by Hawke.

"Have you not learned?!" Theus yelled.

"Listen, I know what you think." Hawke replied. "It isn't what you're expecting."

"What is he talking about, Theus?" Taltus asked.

"Look inside the container. The answer is there."

Taltus looked at the container and saw what Theus saw. A body.

"Nathan, what are you planning?" Taltus now wondered.

"Please tell us what you're truly doing with a body in the container, Hawke?" Nader questioned.

"That body inside the container is the key to defeating Octagon. I call him the Nonagon."

"What's with the numbering?" Mara asked.

"Simple really. Counting."

Upon their conversation, the lab doors opened as The Swordman, Norland, and Fortune returned and with them the quakerium. They were greeted by everyone in the lab, but Hawke's eyes were set on the quakerium.

"What is it, Nate?" Kenari asked.

"I need some of that."

"What for?" Nader wondered. "Are you going to put some of that into your contingency?"

"Look, Octagon's body is made up of solidium. We have no other metal lying around that can stand up to him. But, quakerium, from what I've heard and studied, this mineral has the power and ability to withstand blows from solidium and absorption."

"Hmm." Mara gestured.

"How would it work?" Fortune asked.

"Simple." Hawke replied. "I take a small portion and place it within the chest of the Nonagon. That way, the power of the quakerium will spread throughout the body and he will be able to face Octagon one-on-one."

"And what are we supposed to do while your creations are battling each other?" Nader asked. "Stand by and watch? You have popcorn somewhere in here?"

"Those drones that were scattered earlier aren't the only ones. Octagon has more of them and when the time comes, he will send out word for another challenge. That's where we make things interesting by bringing Nonagon with us."

Kenari grabbed a portion of the quakerium and handed to Hawke. He nodded with respect. Kenari turned and walked away, carrying the rest of the quakerium with him.

"Where are you going?" Fortune asked.

"To put this to good use." Kenari declared. "When Octagon does call, I will be there."

As they were speaking, Hawke placed the quakerium into the container and without a split second to pass the container snapped and shocking bolts of electricity flew from the computer system, rushing inside. Hawke stepped back while the others gazed on. The lightning ceased and the container itself opened and arose from the container was the Nonagon. Rising up like a vampire from his coffin. The eyes of the Nonagon were silent, yet alive. Glowing of golden hue.

"What is it doing?" Nader said.

"He's checking the surroundings." Hawke replied. "Capable of tracking down any possible threats."

Nonagon removed himself from the container, standing

upright on the lab floor, facing everyone. Looking into their eyes, scanning their bodies for any strange anomalies. His eyes were keen toward Taltus and Theus. A glint of red appeared before them.

"Something's not right." Kenari gestured, slowly reaching for his sword.

Nonagon rushed like a flash of light, attacking both Taltus and Theus. He held them by their throats as Norland ran over and tackled the tall, grey android. Fortune attempted to use some of his magic against the android, but they were of no use. Taltus flew and tackled Nonagon against the lab wall, denting it. Theus rushed over as the two held the android to the wall. In doing so, Nonagon's strength was beyond the two strong forces as he busted from their hands and rushed, instantly stopping before Norland, who kicked him into the window and as such, he paused. Stopping and froze. His body turned toward everyone in the lab, he was calm, collective.

"Hawke, control your monster!" Theus said.

Nonagon approached Hawke.

"My creator."

"I am." Hawke replied.

"I can see everything now. The truths of this purpose of my existence."

"I'm not understanding." Norland said. "What does he mean?"

"What I mean is I know why I'm here. For my predecessor."

"You're here to help us take out Octagon." Nader said. "That's why you're here."

"Is it really? I believe there's more to the story than just eliminating my predecessor."

"There is." Hawke said. "You're here to be a protector of mankind."

"A protector."

"Not one of us." Fortune clarified.

"I'm a guardian." Nonagon noticed. "A guardian."

"Yes." Hawke said.

"You have a choice to make." Kenari said, approaching Nonagon. "You can either help us and save lives or face death just like your predecessor."

Nonagon stared into the eyes of The Swordman and nodded. Showing somewhat of a foreign respect.

"I understand." Nonagon replied. "I will help you stop my predecessor from harming lives, and I will be a guardian unto them."

Nonagon stood still as a silvery-grey cape grew from his shoulders, gauntlets formed from his forearms, boots appeared on his feet. All were a silver-grey mixed with a hint of black and white lining. Due to the quakerium, he appeared to have dark purple veins flowing through his body. Kenari nodded and left the lab.

VIII

<u>THE DAY OF OCTAGON</u>

While they sat inside the lab, the screens echoed without a press of a button and upon them was Octagon. His eyes across every screen within the T.I.T.A.N. headquarters. Hawke jumped up as he saw it. Nonagon turned, facing the biggest monitor, staring Octagon in the eye.

"I have chosen to send out this message. I have grown tired of these games, Resistance, Protectors. I believe it is now the time we settle this. Meet me in Newark. The home of my creation and the home of your deaths. Bring all that you can, for this war will be between us and I. For I am. I am."

"He loves to talk doesn't he." Nader gestured.

"This is my day, Resistance. My day, Protectors. My day."

The screens went black as Hawke turned to everyone in the lab.

"Suit up." Hawke commanded.

Everyone prepared, including Nonagon as more armor grew on his body, shining like silver out of the finery. Norland prepared himself, grabbing his helmet, Taltus and Theus went outside as did Nonagon, talking amongst the heroes. Nader prepped his team and Siren joined in on the battle. Fortune spoke with Voltage as they teamed up, already headed out to Newark. Hawke gathered his gear and left.

Over in Newark, Octagon hovered over the city, looking at its structures and the citizens beneath him. He nodded and stretched out his arms with his hands waving over the city.

"This day, they shall know my name. They shall know my purpose. They shall know me."

After a while, the team arrived in Newark and without a sudden notice, Theus pointed up in the sky, Octagon was there, his eyes were keen on them. He flew down to meet them in the streets as the civilians made a run for it. Also, with them was Canadian Hawk, one of Norland's allies. Equipped with his gear.

"Figured we could use an extra hand." Norland said.

"And you picked me out of all the Champions."

Octagon walked toward them on the pavement of the road.

"You've come. But, not all of you. Where my creator? And the Sword-Bearer?"

"Oh, they'll be here." Nader said. "Right now, you'll have to deal with us."

They raised up their weapons toward him and he laughed. Chuckling as he waved his hand toward them in disregard.

"I will not settle for less!" Octagon yelled. "I demand to face my creator!"

From the sky bolted down more Octagon drones, which attacked the heroes. Taltus and Theus took to the skies and battled the raining drones while Norland, Nader,

Hawk, and Siren battled them in the streets. As the fight went on, Octagon stood by and watched.

"Where are you, my creator? Where do you dwell?"

A flash of light emitted from the sky, grabbing all their attention. Octagon looked up and what came down was a large object. Octagon knew what was and he wasn't pleased. Standing up to face it. The object raised its head and it was Nano Man. However, he was not in his current exo-suit as this one was bulkier than his previous suit.

"What have you constructed?" Octagon wondered.

"Call this the Heavy-Duty armor." Nano Man said. "One of my latest projects in work."

A boom echoed through the sky and above them was the sky-rapier and coming down from the fallen rope was The Swordman, decked out in a new armor of his own, equipped and sleeked. Similar to his armor from his first encounter with Taltus. this armor was covered with quakerium.

"Quakerium armor." Octagon said. "Impressive."

"It was the only way to eliminate you." The Swordman declared. "Now is the time."

Also coming from the rapier was Q-Arrow and his aim was set on Octagon. Silver Eagle also made himself known, a portal quickly opened in the streets and from there arrived Fortune, Voltage, and the Beast. Now Octagon was outnumbered.

"This will not be my end." Octagon said. "I am. I am!"

"You are who you've become." A voice said from behind Octagon. "You are what you're end makes you."

Octagon turned around and was standing toe-to-toe with Nonagon. Octagon's eyes were stuck on him. Measuring him and studying him. Seeing its structure inside and out.

"Who are you?" Octagon asked.

"Your successor."

IX

SUCCESSORS

"My-" Octagon said before being tackled by Nonagon into the nearby building.

The battle commenced as The Swordman, Nano Man, Fortune, and Nonagon dealt with Octagon. Q-Arrow, Voltage, and the Beast aided Norland, Nader, Siren, and Hawk on the ground against the running drones. Taltus, Theus, and Silver Eagle faced the aerial drones in the sky. During the battle, Octagon grabbed Nano Man by his throat and threw him into Swordman as he kicked Nonagon to the ground.

"I will not be stopped!" Octagon yelled. "This is my time."

Meanwhile, Q-Arrow fired his arrows toward the drones as Voltage shocked them with his lightning blasts and the finishing blow from the Beast's double-handed smashing. Norland and Hawke double-teamed the drones before being frozen and smashed into pieces. Taltus flew through the drones as if they were paper, Theus summoned a small storm, which snatched the drones from the air and twirled them until they were scattered parts of metal.

Fortune went toward Octagon and blasted him with a magic beam and summoned an energy wire, tying

Octagon's hands together. As such, Nonagon rushed toward Octagon and swiped him, swiping off a portion of his face.

"You dare strike me!"

Octagon snatched Nonagon and choke-slammed him to the pavement, creating a crater in the road. The Swordman ran toward Octagon and began using punches and kicks, in which damaged Octagon's body due to the quakerium. Octagon kicked Swordman back as Nano Man tackled him to the ground and started stomping him repeatedly. Octagon shoved Nano Man from him, as he moved to strike, the Beast hammered Octagon into ground, pounding him until the sounds of cracking went through the area. Octagon's body armor is shattered, and his body begins signaling a shutdown. The Beast roared as he returned to the fight with the others. Nano Man approached the downed Octagon, his helmet opened to reveal his face.

"You think this is the end?" Octagon asked Hawke. "You have no idea what's in store for the future."

"What do you mean?"

"I've seen it and I know the suffering it will bring upon you."

The Swordman approached the downed Octagon and went to impale him with the sword, but Nonagon stopped him.

"Octagon is not yours to eliminate. I will handle him."

"And what will you do?" Fortune asked.

"I will handle him." Nonagon replied. "The others require your assistance. The victory is almost here."

Fortune hovered toward the ongoing battle while Swordman and Nano Man stood next to Nonagon as he placed his foot upon Octagon's chest. Octagon could only chuckle.

"You believe you can replace me?"

"I already have."

"And what will you do once the turn is fixed, and the war is here?"

"What war?" Hawke asked.

"There's a war coming. A great war. There will be smaller wars to take care of before it strikes."

"This is all sounding familiar." Swordman said.

"Let's not." Hawke recommended. "Not right now."

Hawke looked down at Octagon and there was a glint of sadness in his eyes.

"I created you for a purpose. To protect us. To protect this world from those on the other side who deem us harm."

"There is no protecting you from them. It's protecting you from yourselves."

As Octagon spoke to them, the others eliminated the remaining drones and started to celebrate, but there was grief amongst Swordman, Hawke, Nonagon, and Octagon. For what the others did not know, they knew.

Octagon laid his head back as his body was already shutting down from the beatings.

"Finish me off." Octagon told Nonagon. "For this is not the end."

"If it is not the end, when will you return?" Hawke wondered.

"You will know." Octagon replied. "Everyone will know. It will be as a sharp strike upon a country. A horn blowing for war. That day, I will return and with me will be my legion and it will be forever known as the Day of

Octagon."

"We'll be there to stop you." Hawke said.

He gave Nonagon a look as his helmet closed and stepped back. The Swordman followed suit as Nonagon smashed Octagon's body into pieces and ripped out the cerebral interface. Crushing it in his hand. Octagon was defeated.

"It is done." Nonagon said. "I have succeeded my predecessor."

X

FINAL WORDS

Several days later, The Resistance and Protectors went their separate ways. The actions of Octagon were primarily hidden from the rest of the world. T.I.T.A.N. secured the remains of Octagon and brought them to their headquarters. Nonagon went with them and became a guardian over their homestead. Violetress and Rapidshine were taken to a secure location hidden from society. Codenamed '*Hellgate*'.

Elsewhere at Hawke's mansion, both he and Kenari sat together, having a drink. Reflecting on their previous and current battles.

"Did it ever occur to you that we would ever be doing what we're doing?" Hawke asked.

"For me, yes. But, not dealing with corrupted A.I.s. I can deal with the forces from other worlds."

"That's what that sword of yours is for."

Kenari took a sip of his drink.

"Look, you can't disregard the words Octagon spoke. What he said was very similar to-"

"King Stroh." Hawke nodded. "I know and that

worries me."

"Worries you how?"

"Because Stroh gave us a series of events that would unfold before the end. Our battle with the A.I. was the first and that was Octagon."

"And what shall we do to prepare for the next one?"

"What do you propose we do?"

Kenari sat back, thought and nodded with a smile.

"We wait."

Hawke smirked as he took a sip.

"Then wait we shall."

ABOUT THE AUTHOR

Ty'Ron W. C. Robinson II is the author of several works of fiction.
Including the *Dark Titan Universe Saga* series (*Dark Titan Knights,
The Resistance Protocol, Tales of the Scattered, Tales of the Numinous,
Day of Octagon*) and *The Haunted City Saga* series. Also of other books
(*Lost in Shadows, Hod, The Book of The Elect, Symbolum Venatores,
etc.*) and One-Shot short stories More information pertaining to the
author and stories can be found at darktitanentertainment.com.

Twitter: @TyRonRobinsonII
Instagram: @tyronrobinsonii
Podcast: darktitanentertainment.com/podcast
Audiobooks: darktitanentertainment.com/audiobooks
Apparel/Accessories: www.darktitanshop.com
Books: darktitanentertainment.com/books
Newsletter: darktitanentertainment.com/newsletter
Games: darktitanentertainment.com/games